BLOODY GOLD IN YELLOWSTONE

RAYMOND N. KIEFT

BLOODY GOLD IN YELLOWSTONE

YELLOWSTONE MYSTERY SERIES

A PARKER WILLIAMS NOVEL

To order additional copies of this book, contact:
Xlibris
1-888-795-4274
www.Xlibris.com
Orders@Xlibris.com
758480

AUTHOR'S NOTE

As is the case with the previous four novels in the Yellowstone Mystery Series, Bloody Gold In Yellowstone is a work of fiction. Please keep that in mind. If you have read any of my previous novels, you know that I use real places in the greater Yellowstone region of Wyoming, Montana, and Idaho. I also use fictional places. For those readers intimately familiar with the greater Yellowstone region, especially Yellowstone National Park, please be advised that I occasionally use my literary license and tweak geography in favor of storytelling. Geology buffs will excuse the use of gold embedded in small rocks for true veins of gold.

Readers may come across misspelled words, grammatically incorrect phrases, or typographical errors. Excuses are never satisfactory, but here is mine which I trust readers will understand and accept. The less money devoted to the word and grammar editing of this novel by paid professionals means more money for Habitat for Humanity and Compassion International, the two charities which share equally in the royalties earned from the sale of this novel. My excuse is I tried to eliminate all mistakes, as any author would desire, without having a penny diverted from the money going to the two charities. Failing to eliminate all the mistakes, I ask for your indulgence.

Enjoy!

Raymond N. Kieft
ray@raykieft.com
www.yellowstonemysteryseries.com

ACKNOWLEDGMENTS

Very few authors, with the exception of those employing ghost writers, write a novel, especially a fictional novel, without the encouragement of numerous individuals. After the publication of A Watery Grave In Yellowstone, the fourth novel in The Yellowstone Mystery Series, I thought seriously about taking a sabbatical from writing; perhaps even hang it up. To my surprise, I kept receiving inquiries from readers of one or more of the prior Yellowstone Mystery novels asking, "When can I expect to read your next novel?" These inquiries prompted me to not call it quits, at least not yet.

It is dangerous to list individuals who helped me with Bloody Gold In Yellowstone but I would be amiss if I didn't acknowledge one person and convey my appreciation for her assistance. Marti Tanis of Seattle took my first draft and thoughtfully and carefully reviewed it and provided corrections and suggestions which resulted in a much better read than the novel would have been without her assistance.

Raymond N. Kieft

CONTENTS

PROLOGUE

1807

CROW TRIBAL VILLAGE IN THE NORTHERN ROCKY MOUNTAINS NEAR A LARGE LAKE AND RIVER

Chief Swift Eagle looked at the white man sitting cross-legged next to him. He had seen a few other white men but only from a distance. Never this close and never this personal. His nerves were on edge. White men weren't to be trusted. But with ever increasing numbers of white men traveling through Swift Eagle's country, he knew he had to become comfortable with them. He reflected on the circumstances which had brought this one white man into his village and now into his tepee. He had only recently accepted him into the village. He hoped he hadn't made a mistake. He had been very skeptical at first. It was difficult getting beyond past experiences which had caused him to distrust white men. They broke promises, which made Swift Eagle distrust them, at least the white men with whom Swift Eagle had previously come into contact. But, as time passed, he became more comfortable with this particular white man.

Over the past several days, they had shared a pipe while talking about the movement of bison and elk herds. They had also sat in silence, as they were doing now, for long periods of time. This white man seemed comfortable with the ways of the Crow. Since the last full moon, they had eaten together and ridden together surveying the land surrounding the village. They had discussed whether the village should be relocated to new hunting areas. The white man's knowledge of the movement of bison and elk had initially surprised Swift Eagle. It had contributed to Swift Eagle's growing trust in him. What had finally convinced Swift Eagle to trust him was his willingness to join the hunters in their recent bison hunts, share his personal bison kills with the village, and especially give special attention and provide daily care to Running Bear's squaw and daughter. Swift Eagle hadn't asked him to share his kills or provide for Running Bear's squaw and daughter. He had done so on his own. Swift Eagle felt he showed strong medicine by his compassion. Running Bear had been killed when a hunting party, with whom he had been hunting two moons ago, had been ambushed by a marauding band of the hated Blackfoot. The Blackfoot had been defeated but not before Running Bear and three other warriors had been killed. Making this such an ironic hunting party was the capture of the pieces of rock which the Blackfoot had with them. They had taken them from white men coming across their hunting grounds from the place of the great water beyond the mountains. The Blackfoot had killed the white men and taken everything from them. The Blackfoot captured by Swift Eagle's warriors had told the warriors that the pieces of rock had something embedded in them which caused these particular pieces of rock to possess strong medicine. Swift Eagle had seen how white men were eager to trade anything they had, including horses, to obtain only a small number of the pieces of rock. The pieces of rock giving strong medicine were now his and he needed to decide what to do with them. Running Bear and the other warriors should be honored through whatever decision Swift Eagle made. Thinking again about Running Bear's squaw and daughter, he felt remorse since they had been left with no direct means of support. No warrior had come forth voluntarily to provide support. The squaws and children of the other dead warriors were being taken care of by other warriors. The reason for this escaped Swift Eagle. Had Running Bear done something to antagonize his fellow warriors? Did Running Bear's squaw make the other squaws resent her? As was his custom, Swift Eagle waited, for some time, to see if a warrior would come forth to care for Running Bear's squaw and daughter before Swift Eagle would use his authority as chief and direct a warrior to do so. Swift Eagle had been near to choosing a warrior in the village when this white man, who called himself John Colter, had come forth voluntarily to provide the support Running Bear's squaw and daughter needed. Colter had stepped forward before Swift Eagle had to decide which warrior he would direct to provide support for them.

Thinking back, Swift Eagle remembered how he had met John Colter. Colter had been introduced to Swift Eagle by Sacajawea, the squaw who had been with the group of white men on their trip to the great water beyond the mountains. She had told Swift Eagle of John Colter's skill and strength as a hunter and tracker during the travels to and from the great water. At first, Swift Eagle had not allowed Colter into the village. He was a white man, not a Crow. John Colter hadn't been pushy. He had stayed outside the village, entering it only to bring meat to Running Bear's squaw and provide her with two bison hides. He did that only after Swift Eagle had granted approval for him to enter the village. Swift Eagle had watched him ride, track, and hunt, and concluded he rivaled his best warriors. He rode as well as the warriors and had single handedly brought down two bison in a recent hunt. More importantly, he had stood and fought with the other warriors, helping to defeat the warring band of Blackfoot which had attacked the village during the last full moon. Swift Eagle hadn't been able to understand why this John Colter, who was so like his own Crow warriors, didn't join the warriors and celebrate their victory over the Blackfoot by taking wampum. It had to be something white men believed about the spirits of the dead. He dismissed it as white man's medicine. He would never understand it. This combination of warrior-like strength and the thoughtfulness and caring for a dead warrior's squaw and child, while asking nothing in return, had shown Swift Eagle enough to accept John Colter and give him free access throughout the village. Swift Eagle had gone so far as to suggest he reside in Running Bear squaw's tepee. John Colter had declined. Instead, he stayed by himself in his own tepee a short distance outside the village. Another strange custom of white men which Swift Eagle didn't understand.

Looking at John Colter as they sat in silence, Swift Eagle's thoughts were drawn to a piece of birch bark which he kept in a small pouch under his blanket. On the bark was a sketch that he had made. *Can I really trust this white man? Has he really become one of us? What will he do with the piece of birch bark if I give it to him?* Swift Eagle knew if he gave this piece of birch bark to any member of the village, even one of his own children, it would result in jealousy and bring chaos into what was currently a collaborative and peaceful environment. The focus of many men and women of the village would be drawn away from working together for the overall good of the village and instead turn to infighting. The strength of the village lay in its cohesiveness and unity of purpose. Those attributes would be lost if anyone within the village learned the location of the pieces of rock. These pieces of rock constituted strong medicine and Swift Eagle wanted that medicine to be available to his people when they needed it. He now kept one of the pieces of rock in the pouch and would take it out to look at it when no one else was nearby. He could feel strong medicine flowing from it. He had used a piece of birch bark to sketch a drawing showing the location where he had buried the pieces of rock. No one knew the location except himself. He knew his time was soon coming to an end and he would be joining the ancestors in the spirit world. Before he joined the ancestors, he needed to give the piece of birch bark to someone trustworthy who would guard it carefully and only use it to locate the pieces of rock and use them for the benefit of the tribe. The pieces of rock must not fall into the wrong hands. Giving the piece of birch bark to anyone in the village might result in it being captured by the hated Blackfoot or a war party of another enemy tribe if the village was attacked sometime in the future. He sensed the pieces of rock would provide strong medicine for whomever possessed them and he wanted that medicine to be with his people. The location of the pieces of rock needed to remain a secret until they were absolutely needed and then only for the benefit of his Crow brothers and sisters.

He had agonized for several moons trying to decide to whom, if anyone, he would entrust the piece of birch bark. He had almost decided to destroy it before Sacajawea had appeared with the white man. John Colter had proven he was trustworthy. Swift Eagle realized he had found the person to whom he would give his sketch of the location of the pieces of rock.

CROW HISTORY MUSEUM, CROW AGENCY, CROW RESERVATION, MONTANA

Will I ever finish this dissertation? How much longer can I keep pushing? Should I bag this whole thing? I never imagined it would be this much work or take this long. Do I really need to have a Ph.D? Of course, I do. Without it, I won't have a chance to achieve my future goals. I've worked this long and I'm not going to kiss it all off now. I have to keep plugging away. It had already been two years and three months of research, writing, correcting, rewriting, more research; the cycle repeating itself several times. As endless as the process seemed to be and with increasing frustration over the never ending process, Liz still was motivated to locate, analyze, understand, and combine it all into her Ph.D. dissertation. When her dissertation was finally finished, she wanted the academic community to accept it as an important factual history regarding the evolution of federal policies related to mineral rights on land in Wyoming and Montana, much of which was now federally-controlled but initially inhabited by Native Americans. In particular, she had focused her research on policies related to land once inhabited by the Blackfoot and Crow Native American tribes. Her research had necessitated her visiting museums and sites throughout Wyoming and Montana where historical documents were housed regarding the Crow and Blackfoot tribes. She had also been able to review documents housed in the homes of Crow and Blackfoot families and in tribal offices. She had hoped such documents would provide facts and documentation related to her research. She had already reviewed hundreds of documents, many nearly unreadable, examined at least as many photos, often with a magnifying glass. Some were hardly viewable. She had chased down and eventually talked with numerous individuals who were distant relatives of the Native American men and women mentioned in the documents. What had emerged from her work was a hodge-podge of decisions made by numerous federal and state officials and agencies. Some of these decisions were clearly underhanded and illegitimate, resulting in mineral rights being stolen from the Crow and Blackfoot tribes by mining companies from the eastern United States. Personnel of the companies had followed the great western migration of settlers seeking to establish new lives in the West. Unfortunately, paper trails of the actual transactions were very limited. What documents did exist were difficult to decipher. Most were unreadable and not dated. For the most part, they were worthless. At times, it had been all too easy for her to become discouraged. Her discouragement had led her to come close, on several occasions, to abandoning her work, stopping her research, and calling it quits. But, she hadn't quit. She had persevered. Her biggest worry now wasn't what she had documented, but the uncertainty surrounding Professor Boersma. Harold Boersma was her dissertation professor and would essentially determine if her dissertation was accepted. Professor Boersma most often was so involved in his attempt to generate funds for his own research through grant application writing that he showed little interest in whether she was making progress in her own research. Nevertheless, he was her dissertation professor so she had no choice but to keep him informed and trust he would do the right thing and accept her dissertation. Once it was accepted, it would pave the way for her to be awarded a Ph.D.. She fretted whether he would question her ability to analyze and interpret correctly the documents she had been able to read. She was apprehensive that the conclusions drawn from her research might be at odds with the politically correct environment pervading Great Plains University where Professor Boersma was a faculty member and from which her Ph.D. would be awarded. *Will Professor Boersma back me if I'm accused of not being politically correct? Will he abandon me if the going gets tough?* Shaking her head trying to rid herself of her worries, she said to herself, *"I can't worry about him now. I'll cross that bridge if and when I come to it. What will be will be. I've got to keep going. The end is in sight."*

She had spent the weekend pouring over documents she had recently found relating to Chief Swift Eagle and the Crow Native American village he governed. The village had been one of the Crow villages located in northwest Wyoming. Checking with early geographic descriptions and boundary maps developed in the mid 1800s, and comparing them with satellite imaging and using Google Earth, she concluded the village had been located near Lewis Lake and the Lewis Channel in what was now Yellowstone National Park. Knowing the exact location of the village wasn't important. Since Yellowstone encompassed such a vast area, she was confident the village had been located in Yellowstone. If she had interpreted the geographic maps correctly, the satellite imaging placed it in an area of Yellowstone near Lewis Lake and the channel connecting Shoshone and Lewis Lakes . This made sense since access to water was always important for Native American villages. The Lewis River, as well as Shoshone and Lewis Lakes and the numerous smaller streams and creeks flowing into the Lewis River, provided good fishing and hunting. Bison and elk came to the water to drink. She also was aware that wolf research was being conducted in this area. A new pack of wolves had established itself in this area and was now the subject of intensive research into the behavior of a wolf pack which emerged from another pack. The territorial battles between the packs for supremacy were being studied for clues regarding how wolves first established and then protected their territories. At the same time, other research was being conducted on the birth and nurturing of wolf pups by their mothers and the pack. At least one den was known to exist in the area she had identified along the Lewis Channel. It was very well camouflaged and was off limits to everyone, including the wolf research teams. Wolf dens were considered private property of the wolf pack and not to be disturbed, at least until the pups were allowed outside the den.

She was excited about her discovery of the documents attributable to Swift Eagle. He had apparently been a leader who, unlike so many other Native American tribal chiefs, had committed many of his decisions to sketches or marks, usually on pieces of birch bark. Thanks to historians who studied Native American documents, these sketches and marks could be understood as a type of primitive writing. She had located several pieces of birch bark which bore his mark. Fortunately, these pieces were well preserved. Her time spent in educating herself on Native American sketches and markings had been a wise investment since she was able to discern the meaning of them which added to her excitement. In particular, the time she had devoted to educating herself about the sketchings and markings of Crow tribal members had paid off. She had been able to decipher a good deal of Swift Eagle's sketches and markings herself without the assistance of native Crow people. She knew early on she needed assistance if she was to understand fully what Swift Eagle had decided to commit to his sketches and marks. She had hired a native Crow woman to review her interpretations of Swift Eagle's sketches and markings and to translate any of those which Liz hadn't been able to decipher. She also wanted someone to help her with the historical documents related to Swift Eagle and his village, many of which were written by descendants of village members in their own primitive language, based upon oral statements and stories handed down from generation to generation. As she reviewed what the native Crow woman had given her, as well as the historical documents she had obtained for numerous sources, she was impressed with the different strategies Swift Eagle had developed and employed in various battles with the Crow's primary enemy, the Blackfoot. He had obviously been an intelligent leader who wasn't afraid to try new approaches to defending his village. He also employed what would be thought of today as out-of-the-box approaches to growing crops, hunting elk and bison, and building tepees and lodges.

While not a direct focus of her research, she had become fascinated by an aspect of Swift Eagle's leadership which she had never seen before in the governance role of a Native American village chief. Even though it took her away from the main thrust of her research, she had decided to have a diversion and learn more about his view of relationships among the people of his village, especially how he felt about the responsibility of men to take care of widows and orphans whose husbands and fathers had been killed in various battles or in hunting expeditions. She had learned from the Crow woman that Swift Eagle had personally accepted responsibility for the care of several widows and their children. Those to whom he hadn't personally become, what would today be labeled as a step-father or second husband, he directed, ordered was a better word, other men in the village to assume responsibility for them. One fascinating such occurrence, about which she wanted to learn more, had been the care of the widow and daughter of a Crow warrior named Running Bear. He had been killed during an attack by a Blackfoot raiding party. His widow and daughter had become the responsibility of a non-Crow man, actually a non Native American man, who had apparently resided in Swift Eagle's village for a length of time. The only reference Swift Eagle made to him was that he was a white man. A white man residing in a Crow village added to her curiosity. A white man living in a Crow village was something she had never come across or heard about during all her studies and research. If true, it would be a significant discovery. Definitely a feather in her cap. She hadn't been able, so far at least, to decipher the name of the man from any historical document or from what the Crow woman had told her. Perhaps Swift Eagle never did acknowledge the man's name simply because he didn't know it. Not having a name would fly against Native American customs so she was sure the man had been given a name. Maybe she'd get lucky and find his name during her subsequent reading and analysis. *I probably should forget about it since I shouldn't spend valuable time pursuing anything not directly related to my research. But it's interesting and a nice diversion, at least for a little while. Who knows? Perhaps if I can learn more about this guy, I might be able to discover something important about his actions and activities which might provide additional avenues of research for me to pursue once I finish my dissertation.*

INSTITUTE OF NATIVE AMERICAN STUDIES, GREAT PLAINS UNIVERSITY, MADISON POINT, MONTANA

The audacity of the dean to deny my request for funding. Talk about incompetence. This dean takes the prize. Doesn't he understand the importance of my work? My research is head and shoulders above the silly research, I shouldn't even call it research, of the faculty to whom he has awarded funding. Simply outrageous. It was all too obvious. *The dean doesn't understand the importance of my research. He doesn't appreciate the importance of finding and documenting those federal government's policies and actions, during the 1800s, which were related to mineral rights of lands throughout the northern Rocky Mountains once occupied by Native Americans. This isn't something this dean appreciates in the slightest. He simply doesn't comprehend the importance of understanding all aspects of the history of Native American peoples, especially how mistreated many were by the Federal Government.*

He had contemplated going to the student newspaper editor and telling her about how the dean played favorites with friends while discriminating against important research projects devoted to minority interests like those of Native Americans. The student newspaper loved to take on controversial issues and certainly a claim of a dean discriminating against a faculty member would be controversial. But he knew the editor would insist he be identified as the faculty member accusing the dean of discrimination and he couldn't have his name out there because he would forever be blackballed by the university administration. He couldn't afford that happening. No, he had to back away. He had to let it go. He needed to find other sources of funding for his research. *How do such incompetent people like this dean get to be such high ranking administrators with the power of the purse? This guy is unqualified to be a dean. Pure and simple. Okay, so he is a feel good person who doesn't want to raise controversial issues. Those aren't qualities needed in a dean. Added to his groupie-feel approach to administration is his underhanded way of directing research dollars to his friends on the faculty. A total washout.*

His thoughts turned to the graduate students currently engaged in their Ph.D. programs for whom he was their dissertation professor. *Which one or ones have a chance to be awarded grant funds? Who has the best chance of securing funds? If I'm subtle and careful, I could skim off some of the funds from those grants since I'm the professor and they are merely students who are beholden to me. They wouldn't dare confront me. I'm holding all the cards. Now I'm getting somewhere. I can get money from funds obtained by graduate students. That's the way to go. So it wasn't ethical. Too bad. I need the money. Pure and simple. So be it. Nuts to the dean. He can go fly a kite for all I care. Now, which of my graduate students should I concentrate on?* He thought of Elizabeth Buikema. She wasn't his most astute graduate student, but she was determined and a hard worker. He wished she was more of an independent worker and wouldn't bug him so much, but at least she usually had reasonable ideas and not lame brain ones like some of the other graduate students. His thoughts meandered back to thinking about other faculty. Most of them didn't deserve the funds the dean had given to them. But what could he do about it? Nothing, other than obtain funding from other sources. *When I do, I'm going to flaunt it at a future faculty meeting. Watch them all drop their mouths and show their jealousy. I can see it all now. Doctor Harold Boersma has been awarded a multi-year, multi-million dollar grant from the Smithsonian Institute.* He realized he was engaging in fantasy thinking. He was wasting time. *I need to stop thinking about the misguided dean and brown nosing faculty.* He forced his thoughts to return to Elizabeth Buikema or Liz as she preferred to be called.. Her latest activity regarding the Crow tribe was probably going to end up being a big nothing but Harold would let her run with her ideas, at least for a little while longer. He hoped she wouldn't bug him since he needed to get serious and write some proposals for grants to support his own research. He couldn't put all his eggs in the basket of taking funds from grants obtained by graduate students. Liz's recent text to him about the possibility of a white man living in a Crow village was interesting but how did it relate to her research or anything else for that matter? Of course, research was often like that. You didn't always know where it might lead. Perhaps what she was looking into might lead to discovering something important, so he had texted her back telling her to continue pursuing information about this white man. Who knows? Maybe something meaningful would come out of it. If he were lucky, maybe he could turn her findings into cash for himself. After all, he was her research and dissertation professor. He controlled everything related to her research and the ultimate approval of her dissertation. If she found some historic artifact or document, which collectors would pay dearly to obtain, even if it meant working the black market, he could probably turn it into cash. Of course, he would share the cash with Liz. Not a 50-50 split. Probably a 75-25 split. After all, without him, she wouldn't have a prayer of being awarded a Ph.D. and that was worth money, wasn't it? *Enough of my dreaming. What I really need to do is to forget about the myopic vision of the dean and the pie-in-the-sky dream of Liz discovering something which I can turn into money for myself. I need to get my act together and get busy preparing proposals for grants in case my strategy to obtain funds from graduate students doesn't pan out.*

TRAVELING THE WEST ENTRANCE ROAD, YELLOWSTONE NATIONAL PARK, WYOMING

He was antsy. It was time to move on. He was looking forward to the end of this job and moving on. Driving one of the famous yellow tour buses of Yellowstone National Park had been fun in the beginning but it had quickly become drudgery. Sure, Yellowstone was beautiful. Yes, the abundance of geysers, thermal features, waterfalls, and wildlife was amazing. But the never ending idiotic questions from tourists had finally gotten to him. The latest idiotic question - "when do the deer become elk?" - had pushed him over the edge and nearly caused him to lose it. He had bitten his tongue and answered as if the question wasn't stupid. The ignorance of people was appalling. He had to move on. He probably would have bagged this job already if it wasn't for Liz. Liz. Liz the dreamer. Liz the do-gooder. Trying to show how Indians had been shafted by the Feds. So, what else is new? The Feds have always shafted people. The whole tax structure was one big shaft. Yes, good ole Liz. Smiling to himself, he thought how Liz was going to be his cash cow. She was going to be his ticket out of this drudgery. Somehow, he was going to gain her confidence. He was going to convince her he was fascinated with her and wanted a caring relationship. Truth be told, he couldn't care less about a relationship, at least a relationship which lasted past using her to accomplish his own ends. Nevertheless, he needed to get closer to her and quickly. He wished she wasn't gone for such long periods of time. It bothered him because he couldn't work on his plan to gain her confidence and establish a closer relationship if she was absent so much. He needed her close for his plan to work. He knew she had money, plenty of money it seemed. In a weak moment, she had told him about her money and how more would keep coming for a considerable time. Good ole trusting Liz. She had told him about a trust she had from her grandparents. She told him she received a lump sum annually plus a monthly stipend. Unfortunately, she hadn't told him all the details about her receipt of funds. He knew enough to know that if he played his cards right, he could access quite a bit of her money, at least enough to enable him to move on and support himself for awhile. With a sizable bank roll, he could disappear and live frugally for a long time. One thing for sure, no more doing grunt work. No more dealing with ignorant people. Those days would be history.

He knew her research was behind her absences . *Silly stuff,* he thought to himself. "*Who cares about how Indians were treated over mineral rights? Everyone knows Indians were shafted. Why doesn't she forget about such foolish stuff?*" The last he knew, she was currently on the Crow reservation doing research on the Federal Government's policies regarding mineral rights for the Crow tribe. She seemed to him to be too emotional about her research. It was as if she herself was a member of the Crow tribe. The health of the tribe didn't depend on her discovering and documenting how the Federal Government had cheated the tribe out of its rights to the minerals throughout the land once held by the tribe. He had to convince her to place more emphasis on building their relationship and less on her research. Not seeing her as often as he wanted and needed added to his feelings of desperation. He needed time with her to gain her confidence and build a more trusting relationship, at least her trusting him more. Once she trusted him more, he could work on getting her money. There wasn't much time remaining. He simply couldn't face those idiotic tourists for much longer.

Pulling into the parking area by the Middle Geyser Basin, he explained to the riders about the mud pots and geysers they would see. He told them to make sure they stayed on the boardwalk and didn't venture off it. Every year, a few tourists didn't follow the admonition to stay on marked trails and the consequences were often tragic. Every so often, he heard about a tourist falling through the thin crust surrounding geysers and other thermal features. With the water around the thermal features at boiling temperature, anyone falling through the crust was quickly boiled to death. Not a pleasant way to go.

After the last person left the bus, he leaned back, placed the ear buds of his iPod into his ears, and settled back to listen to one of his favorite tunes while he thought more about getting a sizable portion of Liz's money. The more he thought about it the more he realized he'd do whatever it took to get her money. *I guess I have to go to her, wherever she is, and work my magic. I can't achieve my goal if I'm not around her. I need to find her. Pure and simple. I need to get money from her. I will get it, whatever it takes. Then good ole Aaron Vogelzang will be on his way.*

GOLD MEDAL FLY FISHING SHOP, WEST YELLOWSTONE, MONTANA

The water levels in the numerous rivers and streams in the Yellowstone region had dropped to where wading was no longer dangerous. Float boats were no longer being swept along so rapidly by the surging currents that fishing from them wasn't possible. The spring and early summer run-off from melting snow in the surrounding mountains, which provided the water for all the thermal features in Yellowstone, as well as the rivers and streams throughout the Park, had cleared, resulting in crystal clear water. The combination of clear water and normal currents made conditions ideal for fly fishing. Yellowstone and the surrounding area were known as the fly fishing capital of the lower forty-eight. Nowhere else were so many productive fly fishing rivers, streams, and lakes located so close together and so accessible. No other area came close to offering the plethora of fly fishing opportunities. One indication of the area's reputation rested on the fact that no less than six full service fly fishing retail establishments called West Yellowstone home. In the surrounding area, additional fly fishing shops could be found. In the heart of this fly fishing mecca was the Gold Medal Fly Fishing Shop, located in West Yellowstone.

The fly fishing guides employed by Parker Williams, owner of the shop, were booked for several days. Fly fishers from across the country flocked to the Yellowstone region to test their fly fishing skills while basking in the splendor and beauty of Yellowstone National Park. It was not unusual for the shop to have clients from California, Texas, Illinois, Florida, and New York the same day. This was the time of the year when merchants in West Yellowstone made their living which had to last them throughout the times when visitors to Yellowstone slacked off.

Business had been humming all morning in the shop. Parker was doing all he could to keep the inventory of fishing flies fully stocked. The inventory seemed to decrease as quickly as he could restock it. As usual, the fishing flies most commonly known among fly fishers were the best sellers even when the fish were eating something else and were ignoring these commonly known fishing flies. Why fish, especially trout which had been born in the wild and lived in the wild their entire lives, concentrated on eating one insect rather than others, when many eatable insects were present in the water in equal numbers, mystified experts and amateurs alike. Why fish ate what they did at various times and ignored all other food had been for many years an area of study by fishery and wildlife researchers and professionals. Parker and the guides of the shop had their own ideas about the reasons for such action by the trout throughout Yellowstone. When they thought they had figured it out, the trout would act entirely different. They then had to go back to the drawing board to start all over and form new theories and investigate other possibilities. Parker sometimes thought the way trout chose to eat was as simple as how people acted at a buffet; people chose different foods in no particular pattern and ignored other food based upon color, size, smell, taste, past eating experiences, curiosity, and probably many other reasons. Trout seemed to act similarly.

With his fly fishing business well organized and going full steam, Parker had some time to consider aspects of the business he had for too long ignored. For instance, he knew he needed to employ another guide or two to make sure no client was turned away. A potential client not served was probably going to be a person who never came back. Worse yet, a disappointed person would probably tell another potential client about her or his disappointment. When he did employ more guides, he realized one, if not all, needed to be a woman. More and more women across the United States had become fly fishers and their numbers continued to increase. Fly fishing was no longer a male dominated sport. All one had to do was flip through a fly fishing catalog to see the equipment and clothing now being manufactured and marketed for women. In the past, some of the women clients had expressed being anxious about being with a male guide and feeling vulnerable when they were a distance from any other person when fishing a river or stream. Parker trusted all his male guides. If there was ever an incident involving a woman client, that guide would be let go and possibly turned over to the authorities. Thankfully, nothing had ever happened and Parker didn't want it to ever happen.

The feelings of vulnerability were real to women clients. To address this, Parker had begun to only accept a woman client when a male companion, either her husband, significant other, brother, or male friend she trusted, went with her, either as a client himself or just an observer. This arrangement had worked in the past since not many women had requested a guide. That had all changed with the growing number of women who were now established fly fishers, many without a male to accompany them when they requested a guide. Some of these women specifically requested a female guide. Lori Black had stepped in the breach on occasion and provided guide services but it wasn't her cup of tea and, if truth be told, she wasn't very good at it. Her role was in the shop where she was Parker's most valued employee. In reality, she managed the shop. He thought to himself, "*Sure, I'm the owner and in charge, but Lori really runs the show. She and her mother keep the shop humming. Having Lori guide, even only occasionally, isn't the answer. I must hire at least one female guide and more if possible.*"

He knew what he would do to find women to hire as potential guides. He would contact Beth. Beth Richardson was the Assistant Superintendent of Yellowstone National Park. She was the highest ranking official of the U.S. Interior Department holding a position in a national park in the western United States. He would ask her to inquire of the Human Resources Department about women, who applied for positions with Yellowstone in either fishery science or wildlife management, but hadn't been hired. Chances were such women, since they had an interest in working in Yellowstone in some capacity related to fish or wildlife, would have some knowledge and experience in the outdoors. *If I'm lucky, there may be a woman or possibly two women with fly fishing experience who could become certified as fly fishing guides.* The certification process had been developed by the Professional Guide Association as a means to keep unscrupulous and fly-by-night people from claiming they were guides without knowing the first thing about fly fishing and especially fly fishing in Yellowstone with its special regulations. He would be willing to pay the fee associated with the certification process if he found the right woman or women. *That's what I'll do. I'll call Beth. Besides, I want to catch up with her. I don't want her to think I've lost interest in her. It's just the opposite. I feel badly neglecting our friendship. Whom am I kidding? If I'm honest with myself, Beth means a lot more to me than just a friend, a whole lot more.* Beth and he had engaged in an on-again, off-again relationship for the past few years. The chemistry was certainly there, no doubting that. When they were together, they both said they enjoyed it and wanted to build upon it. They had been intimate, but always cautious to limit their intimacy. When they seemed to be progressing toward a more serious and in-depth relationship, one or both of them would back away. Both of them cited the responsibilities of their work and career as curtailing further involvement, but Parker knew, at least in his case, there were other factors. His rejection by his former wife still weighed on him which caused him to be overly cautious about entering into a deeper, long-term relationship with a woman. Taking his mobile phone and scrolling through his contacts, he found Beth's office and mobile phone numbers. *Probably best to call her office. She could be in a meeting and would most likely have her mobile phone turned off.* He pressed the "call" button for Richardson, Beth, office. After three rings, a male answered. Parker recognized the voice as Larry Noorlag, Beth's administrative assistant. "Assistant Superintendent Richardson's office, Larry speaking."

"Hi, Larry. It's Parker Williams. Might Beth be available?"

"I'll check, Doctor Williams. One moment, please."

Parker smiled, assuming Larry knew whether Beth was available to talk but didn't want to commit her to doing so without first obtaining her permission. It was known as call screening. Parker recalled having the same arrangement in his office as president of a university. With call screening, he remembered his assistant would tell him who was calling. He could then decide if he wanted to talk or didn't want to talk with the individual calling. If he didn't, his assistant would tell the caller he wasn't available.

"Hi, Parker. How nice to hear from you. Its been much too long. Is this a social or business call?"

"Hi, Beth. Both, I guess," replied Parker. "It has been too long and I apologize for being so inconsiderate. I miss you Beth. Pure and simple. I miss you. Before we end this call, I want to agree on a definite time to get together."

"If you've been inconsiderate, so have I. I miss you too. How about a picnic in the next day or two? The weather forecast is good. We could meet half way, say at the picnic area by Tower Falls. I'll take the afternoon off. I have quite a bit of vacation time I haven't used. What do you say?"

"I say you're on. Tower Falls at noon. I'll bring everything. You just bring yourself."

"Wow! How can a girl turn this one down? I'll be there. Now, what is the business reason for your call?"

"I'm hoping you can help me. I need to hire at least one more fly fishing guide, specifically a woman guide. I thought you might be aware of women who applied for positions in fishery or wildlife management with Yellowstone but, for whatever reasons, weren't hired. If any are still in the area, I could contact them if you would give me names and contact information. Maybe one or possibly two might be able to serve as a fly fishing guide."

"I may not have to do any of that since I know someone who would be ideal for you. Right now, she's volunteering in my office. She's my cousin's daughter. My only cousin who is like a brother. She's waiting for a position to open with Todd Meninga in fishery management. She majored in fishery science at Boise State and I know she fly fishes. I can ask her to contact you. I'm late for a meeting. See you at Tower Falls at noon. Don't forget the wine."

"See you then and there. Have your cousin's daughter contact me. Don't worry, I won't forget the wine. And thanks."

CROW HISTORY MUSEUM, CROW RESERVATION, CROW AGENCY, MONTANA

She was excited. She had discovered the name of the white man who lived in Swift Eagle's village. A famous explorer and mountain man who had been a member of the historic Lewis and Clark exploration team. John Colter. He was the non-Native American who had lived among the Crows in Swift Eagle's village. This was an important historical discovery and she owned it. However, she didn't know how much more time she should spend searching for more materials related to John Colter's time with Swift Eagle's Crow village. Every minute spent researching this meant less time on her primary goal of successfully completed her research and finishing her dissertation. She had to admit she was fascinated by how Colter had apparently become a full-fledged member of the village and had been involved with a particular squaw and her daughter, although she had found no evidence of what would be a marriage or even a live-in situation of the squaw and Colter. *I really need to put this aside and get back to my dissertation and my research on the mineral rights of the Crows. I can always return to investigating this aspect of Colter's life later. But, I still want to interview that Crow woman in the nursing home. I went to interview her last week but couldn't see her because she was ill. Once I talk with her, I'll set aside my interest in John Colter and the Crow village until after I complete my dissertation.*

She reflected on what she had discovered in addition to learning about John Colter. She had been reading through some historical documents and had come across the name of a Crow woman which had triggered a remembrance of the same name being included in articles about Swift Eagle's village. Doing some research using Google and Ancestry.com, she had verified a woman, currently living in a nursing home on the Crow reservation, had the same last name as the woman mentioned in one of the articles. Given what Liz understood about names in the Native American culture, these two women were most likely related, the earlier being an ancestral relative of the currently living woman. Liz realized it was a long shot but the woman in the nursing home might be able to shed some light on happenings in Swift Eagle's village if her ancestral relative had shared her experiences with other relatives. One or more of these relatives may have passed them down to this woman in the nursing home. *I'm going to try one more time to talk to this Crow woman. She might not have anything useful to share with me but I won't know unless I try.* With this in mind, Liz gathered up her papers, stuffed them into her attache along with her laptop and phone. She exited the museum and walked to her Nissan pick-up truck. Starting it, she drove from the parking lot to highway 310 and headed for the Peaceful Waters nursing home on the other end of the Crow Reservation.

Entering the nursing home, Liz inquired if Beverly Conner was still a resident and if she could have visitors. The attendant inquired regarding Liz's interest in visiting with Mrs. Conner. Liz told the attendant about her research project and the article about Swift Eagle's village. She said the article mentioned a woman named Many Waters which, Liz believed, was the name of an ancestor of Mrs. Conner. Liz assured the attendant she was only interested in learning from Mrs. Conner anything she might recall being told by her mother, grandmother, or great-grandmother about life in Swift Eagle's Crow village in the early 1800s. The attendant told Liz that if Mrs. Conner agreed, Liz could visit with her. Her visit could be no longer than ten to fifteen minutes as Mrs. Conner tired easily and could become irritable and upset. The attendant stressed that if Mrs. Conner became upset, Liz's visit would be terminated immediately. Finally, Liz was told no photos were allowed and she could not make a recording of her visit because privacy concerns were paramount for the protection of the residents.

Agreeing to everything, Liz was told to wait. The attendant left her and returned a few minutes later. "Mrs. Conner is awake and said she would see you. Please remember, no more than ten or fifteen minutes. Then I'll come to escort you from the building. Please follow me."

Liz was escorted down a hall with rooms on each side. When they reached Room 23, the door was slightly open. The attendant indicated Liz should walk into the room. Entering the room, Liz saw an elderly woman, obviously of Native American heritage, sitting in a chair looking out her window. Knowing the proper greeting to a elderly Native American woman was *grandmother*, Liz said, "Good afternoon, grandmother."

Turning her head to look at Liz, the elderly woman answered, "Good afternoon, child. Nurse Singing Rain said you wish to talk with me. Have you been here before? Have we talked before?"

"No, grandmother, I haven't been here before. We have never talked. I'm doing research on the history of your people. May I visit with you for awhile?"

"I don't know you but they wouldn't have let you in to see me if they didn't believe you were harmless. I don't know what they're so worried about all the time. Who wants to hurt a bunch of old people? We have nothing anybody wants. All we have is memories. You want to discuss my people. What about my people? Why is a white woman, a young one at that, interested in my people? Oh, I'm getting ahead of myself. After you answer a question I have for you, I'll decide if I want to talk with you. What in particular about my people do you want to talk with me about? You said you are doing research on the history of my people."

"Grandmother, I'm particularly interested in Chief Swift Eagle's village. I would very much like to know what you remember your mother, grandmother, great-grandmother, or anyone else for that matter, telling you about your people's life in Chief Swift Eagle's village."

Liz saw the woman stiffen at the mention of Swift Eagle. *Why the reaction? Have I touched a nerve? I'd better be careful what I say and how I say it.* Sitting forward in her chair, Mrs. Conner replied in a surprisingly stern voice, "Are you going to use whatever I might tell you for the good of my people or for your own good? My people have been taken advantage of much too often. I don't want to be taken advantage of either. Even though I'm old, I can still read people fairly well. You seem to be an honest girl. I want your promise that whatever I tell you won't be used against my people. If you promise, I think we can continue to visit. I don't get many visitors these days, so I would enjoy being with you. My grandson and his friend come by once in awhile but they only stare at their phones. A terrible thing those smart phones, if you ask me. What is so smart about them? They isolate people even more. Is that smart given all the problems we have in our world between people?"

"Grandmother, I promise you, whatever you tell me will in no way be used against your people. I must tell you, however, that I might use what you tell me to further my research and help me obtain my Ph.D. degree. So yes, it may be for my own good as well."

"How refreshing. Honesty. See, I sized you up correctly. You are honest. Now, let's get past this grandmother stuff. My name is Beverly Conner. My husband's name was Luke, Luke Conner. He passed several years ago. Before I was married to him, my name was Beverly Many Waters. What is your name?"

Trying hard to contain her excitement in verifying the ancestral connection of the woman, Liz responded, "My name is Elizabeth Buikema. People call me Liz. May I can you Bev?"

"Liz and Bev it is. Now, let's get to the point of your request. These people here don't allow me to visit with anyone very long. They say I get tired. That's baloney, but what can I do about it? They don't ask me if I'm tired. I think that they're lazy and don't want to bother with me. So, what do you wish to know about Swift Eagle's village?"

Surprised by her directness, Liz felt she could get right to the point. "Bev, I believe you had ancestors or ancestral relatives living in the village of Chief Swift Eagle. I have discovered an explorer and mountain man named John Colter spent time in the village. It seems he actually became a member of Swift Eagle's village and was involved with a widowed squaw and her daughter. Does any of this ring a bell with you?"

A look came over Bev's face which Liz couldn't decipher. Something told Liz she had struck a nerve. What could it be? "You are not the first person who has asked me about what I remember being told about Swift Eagle's village. I have to tell you I can't be so sure what I remember and what I don't. Let me talk and you will have to sort out fact from fiction, I'm afraid. Do you have a recorder? They don't want you to have one but it's okay with me if you do. They run this place like there are secrets here. What secrets can a bunch of old people have?"

"I do have a recorder. Since it's okay with you, I'd like to use it." Opening her laptop case, Liz withdrew a small hand-held recorder. Switching it on, she said, "I'm all set if you are."

"My mother told me her great-grandmother, who would be an ancestral relative of mine, lived in the village you are talking about, one where Swift Eagle was chief. Yes, she mentioned a white man came to live in the village. He became a trusted friend of Swift Eagle. I don't recall my mother telling me this white man's name or anything about being involved with a widowed squaw . If this man was John Colter, I can't say. I do recall being told this white man gave several keepsakes to a daughter of a warrior named Running Bear. He had been killed by the Blackfoot. As I recall, this daughter of Running Bear married a white man named Sanders. My mother once told me descendants of this daughter of Running Bear had Sanders as their last name. Of course, with all these hyphen names these days, who knows about family names anymore. Anyway, she said they lived on a ranch outside Livingston. That's it. I've told you what I remember. That's what I remember being told about Swift Eagle's village and a white man who was a friend of Swift Eagle. You say the man was an explorer named John Colter. I know nothing about a John Colter. As I said, according to what I remember being told, whoever this man was, he was trusted by Swift Eagle and became a good friend of my people."

Liz couldn't believe what she had just learned. If what she had just heard was true, it meant she could pursue finding more information about the daughter of Running Bear and her descendants which, in turn, could provide information about John Colter and Swift Eagle. Her excitement grew as she realized this would be new historical information. It would open a whole new line of research about Colter's life and the Native American people with whom he interacted when he was in the Yellowstone region. Learning more about Colter, his involvement with the Crow tribe, and, in particular, his living in Swift Eagle's village, could result in a bonanza in terms of history which hadn't yet been discovered, let alone published. With such new information to add to what she had already identified, she would be assured of earning her Ph.D. She realized she had to pursue what she had learned today. She had to determine if Bev recalled facts or had fabricated stories which had been embellished as made-up stories often were. Liz realized she might be on the brink of something very big if Bev's story checked out. "Bev, your memory is very good. You said the daughter of Running Bear married a man named Sanders. Do you remember anything more about them? Are there Sanders still living in the Livingston area? You mentioned keepsakes being given to Running Bear's daughter by the white man who may or may not have been John Colter. Do you recall your mother saying anything about those keepsakes?"

Again, Liz saw Bev stiffen and a look come across her face which Liz couldn't decipher. "Sorry, Liz, but what I've told you is all I recall. If you want to look for more information, you might go to Livingston and dig into the records regarding a Sanders family. As for keepsakes, I don't recall my mother telling me anything about them. If I was told any specifics or details, I don't remember. My mother either never told me what the keepsakes were or I've forgotten what she told me."

"Bev, I know the government mistreated your people and other Native American tribes. Your people were lied to and promises to your people were broken. Treaties with your people weren't honored and they were forced from their lands and ignored. Maybe through my research and the publication of my findings more people will become aware of the truth regarding the heritage of your people. All my work would be worth it if that was the result." Looking out the door and down the hall, Liz continued, "I see a nurse coming. I suspect she is going to tell me I have to leave." Switching off the recorder, she placed it back into the laptop case. Taking Bev's hand, she said, "We won't have any more time to talk now so I'd like to come back to continue our conversation. Could I come again, Bev?

After she was sure Liz wouldn't be coming back to her room, Bev told Nurse Singing Rain she wanted to nap and asked to have the door of her room closed. Now that she was alone, she had no intention of sleeping. Far from it. Her visit with Elizabeth Buikema had been stimulating but also troubling. She seemed to be a nice young woman with intent on causing no harm. She seemed sincere in wanting to help the Crow tribe but wasn't that what white people had been saying for years and years? Reflecting on their conversation, Bev regretted telling Liz as much as she had. She had lost track of herself in the give and take about Swift Eagle. She never should have said what she had to Liz especially about keepsakes being given to Running Bear's daughter. But Liz seemed to be genuinely interested in helping and Bev had gotten carried away with telling her about Swift Eagle. She realized she had made a mistake. She knew what she had to do. She again checked to make sure she was alone and the door to her room was closed.

Opening the drawer of the nightstand next to her bed, she found the phone. These smart phones were a nuisance but she knew the world now used and relied on them. Almost everyone in the nursing home had one even though only a few of the residents knew how to use them. Bryson Yellow Feather had given the phone to her and was even paying the monthly service cost. Not a bad deal. He said he wanted her to be able to contact him or any of his family members if she needed something which the nursing home didn't or wouldn't provide. He was one of the few young men who still cared about the elderly. He was also loyal to the heritage of the tribe. She knew he was engaged with a few other young tribal men in searching for historical records which could be used to pressure the Bureau of Indian Affairs to better support the tribe. What it was he thought he would find to help the tribe was lost on her. Nevertheless, she found his enthusiasm and commitment refreshing given the lack of motivation of most of the young men of the tribe. All they wanted to do was sit around, drink beer, and stare at their phones. She had hardly contacted Bryson at all since she didn't want to bother him. Besides, what was an old woman going to talk about with a young man? Where this Buikema woman could be headed and potentially what she might discover was too great a risk to be brushed aside as just another white woman trying to do good for the poor, down and out Indians. In particular, Bev knew Bryson and his team of young men had been engaged in trying to determine if there was truth to the story handed down orally from generation to generation about Swift Eagle and the pieces of rock with gold in them which he had discovered. If Liz was as honest as she seemed to be, perhaps she could join Bryson's team, even though she wasn't a Crow. Bev would leave that up to Bryson to decide. Her task was to alert him to what Liz asked about and where she might be headed.

Bryson's phone number was already in her phone. When he had given her the phone, he had made sure she knew how to locate his number and press the "call" button, which she now did. He answered after the third ring. "Hello. This is Bryson."

"Bryson, it's Grandma Conner. I want you to know about a conversation I just had with a young white woman who is digging into the life of Swift Eagle."

CROW RESERVATION, CROW AGENCY, MONTANA

The information Grandma Conner had shared with him prompted him to call an emergency meeting of his investigative team. He clued them in about Elizabeth Buikema. He also described his plan for dealing with her. *White people continually want to help us poor, downtrodden, helpless Indians. What can't they understand? We don't want their help. Our bottom line is they need to keep their noses out of our business.* His team had concurred with his assessment of the risk this Buikema woman posed. After fiercely debating an ultimate outcome, should she prove to be obstinate and uncooperative, team members had agreed with his plan for eliminating Elizabeth Buikema, should it be necessary to do so.

Thank goodness he had stayed in touch with Grandma Conner and shown her the respect the elderly of the tribe deserved. Sure, she was living in the past and wasn't a participating member of the Crow nation any longer. Nevertheless, there were some things in their people's heritage that you honored and treated with respect. The elderly was one. What Grandma Conner had told him about the white woman set off alarm bells. He and his team were too close to nailing down the location of the pieces of rock Swift Eagle had hidden, at least that was the story which had been passed down from generation to generation and had been motivating their efforts for the past several months. The story was that Swift Eagle and his warriors had defeated a band of Blackfoot which had, in their possession, pieces of rock embedded with gold. Swift

Eagle had gone on to bury the pieces of rock somewhere near a lake and a river or stream in what was now Yellowstone National Park. This story was repeated over and over again and passed down from Crow generation to the next generation. Bryson realized it might all be a feel good story with no truth to it. Because this story had been handed down from generation to generation without anyone being able to verify its veracity, it might only be that – a story with no basis in fact. A story shared around campfires to make tribal members feel hopeful that some day, some dedicated member of the tribe would come across a clue to prove the story was indeed true and the pieces of rock were still where Swift Eagle had hidden them.

The clue, if it existed, had to be something which Swift Eagle had produced. Hopefully, a sketch or some marks providing sufficient detail to give Bryson and his team enough information to narrow down the possibilities of the location of the pieces of rock. There were more than five hundred streams, creeks, and rivers throughout the Yellowstone region, many near lakes, big and small, many several miles in length and many located in very remote and rugged terrain. There were numerous canyons, some small and others large and deep, like the Lewis River canyon and the Grand Canyon of the Yellowstone River, both located near lakes. It was impossible to investigate them all. It would take his team years to cover the Yellowstone landscape without having any information to narrow down the possibilities. It simply wasn't feasible. They needed a break. Something to narrow down the possibilities. What he did know is they didn't need a white woman sticking her nose into their business.

Since Elizabeth Buikema had asked Grandma Conner about a white man named John Colter residing in Swift Eagle's village, it had added credibility to the story about Swift Eagle and the pieces of rock. Bryson respected Swift Eagle as a leader. Why Swift Eagle had embraced a white man was baffling. *What if Swift Eagle told John Colter about the pieces of rock and now Elizabeth Buikema is investigating what went on between Swift Eagle and Colter? Has she already discovered some information about Swift Eagle and Colter which would help me in narrowing my search? Who knows, maybe she has already discovered whether Swift Eagle told this Colter fellow about the pieces of rock and worse yet, their hidden location. She may be ready to go to the location and make a claim for the gold. If the location is within the boundary of the national park, the gold will, most likely, be claimed by the U.S. Government. I can't let that happen. Those pieces of rock and the gold in them belong to my people.*

Realizing he had to confront her and find out what she knew or what she was planning, he decided he would do a Google search of Elizabeth Buikema. The information he learned would help him discover where she was living and how best to confront her. Grandma Conner had told him she was doing research for her dissertation which meant she was enrolled as a graduate student. *She's probably enrolled in a masters or doctoral program in one of the universities in the area. I'll also do a search of the graduate programs of these universities and see if any relate to the history of Native Americans, especially the Crow Tribe. I'll then go and confront her. If she isn't forthcoming, I'll be ready to make her share what she knows and is planning. If it takes some heavy duty persuasion, so be it. My ancestors used torture on white people and since it was good enough for them, it is good enough for me. Once I learn what she knows and what information she wants, I'll make sure she doesn't follow through. No one is going to steal what is ours.*

TWO WEEKS LATER
GOLD MEDAL FLY
FISHING SHOP, WEST
YELLOWSTONE, MONTANA

She had been very enthusiastic about becoming a fly fishing guide and her enthusiasm hadn't waned. Maybe her enthusiasm had something to do with the Gold Medal Fly Fishing Shop, at least Parker hoped it did. Gretchen was everything Beth had told him; experienced in fly fishing and knowledgeable about the particulars of fly fishing in Yellowstone. Over a short period of time, she had distinguished herself and earned a reputation for competency, pleasing personality, and a helping attitude and approach to beginning women fly fishers. She had served as a guide for several women clients, all of whom had given her a substantial gratuity indicating their pleasure with her service. She was a keeper as far as Parker was concerned. Not only because of her fly fishing moxie but also because she was Beth's cousin's daughter and Beth had adopted her, so to speak. Beth and Gretchen's father were very close, much like having a sister-brother type relationship. Consequently, Beth treated Gretchen much as a mother would treat a daughter. There was only one drawback with Gretchen, at least from his perspective, and it worried him. She was obsessed with money. She talked about it a great deal. She had told him her goal was to be rich. He passed it off as a young woman's fantasy. Nevertheless, it troubled him since he had known people who acted foolishly and sometimes harmfully when obsessed with acquiring money.

Having someone in his employ who was close to Beth couldn't help but enhance his relationship with her. Also, he wanted, in an indirect way, to do something nice for Beth. Gretchen was driving everyday back and forth from Grant Village to the shop, some thirty-six miles one way. Since Beth was a high ranking official within the Yellowstone hierarchy, she was furnished a Chevy Tahoe. Consequently, she had lent Gretchen her personal Honda CR-V to use. The miles on the CR-V were piling up and Parker wondered how much longer it would be before Beth realized the wear and tear on her CR-V were adding up and eventually she might have to replace parts, especially tires, and make repairs. He wasn't going to say anything to Beth right now since Gretchen could do no wrong in Beth's eyes. Gretchen was fair-haired and walked on water as far as Beth was concerned.

Gretchen was living in Grant Village with a college roommate, who was conducting research in pursuit of her Ph.D. degree. They shared a housekeeping cabin with a small kitchenette and two tiny bedrooms. Most people would label such a cabin as primitive. it was primitive when compared to the hotels and motels proliferating across the country. Nevertheless, it seemed to fit the two women well. Beth had pulled a few strings, Parker assumed, in order for the cabin to be reserved indefinitely, which was against Yellowstone's housing policy. Cabins in Yellowstone were in high demand and the policy stated no one could reserve a cabin for more than two weeks. The cabin then had to be vacated and subsequently be assigned to someone else. This policy had been implemented several years earlier when it become clear too many visitors were unable to obtain lodging in the park because other visitors were reserving cabins for long time periods. According to what Gretchen had told Parker, Elizabeth Buikema was her roommate's name. She was, for substantial periods of time, away from Grant Village conducting research on the Crow reservation. The two women did keep in touch via texts and occasional phone conversations, especially if something demanded their attention. Their respective activities meant they were away from each other and the cabin for a majority of time. It probably contributed to their cooperative living arrangement.

Gretchen had called Parker at his home last evening to ask him if it was okay that she not come to the shop the following day. She did not have a client to guide and Liz was coming back from the Crow reservation with something special she wanted to show Gretchen. Even though he could have used her in the shop to give Lori some assistance, he had told Gretchen it was okay to not come in. A shipment of Sage fly fishing rods and reels had arrived late the previous afternoon and Dick Wells, Parker's longtime employee and fly tier extraordinaire, was currently checking each rod and reel for any manufacturing defects before signing off on the delivery and sending a cashier's check to Sage. Dick was Parker's longest tenured employee, having been the first employee Parker hired when the fly fishing shop was opened. Dick was a jack-of-all-trades. He served as a guide, sales person, inventory manager, and advertising agent. Above all, he was a fly tier of immense talent. He tied all the specialty fishing flies for the shop. He had a serious reputation throughout the fly fishing community which resulted in fly fishers across the country ordering flies tied by Dick. Each year, more of Dick's flies were ordered and this aspect of the business was now a major revenue stream. A couple of his flies had been featured in *Fly Fisherman* magazine which resulted in hundreds of orders coming from across the country.

Parker was thankful for Dick's versatility and his careful assessment of the quality of merchandise the shop purchased from various manufactures for sale to customers. For example, at approximately $1,000 per rod and reel, it was important to make sure each Sage rod and reel were free of defects before paying for them. It was rare to find any defect with any product manufactured by Sage. The company maintained a rigorous quality control process and only very rarely did anything slip through the cracks. Nevertheless, a defect could occur and Parker didn't want to be the recipient of a defective fly fishing rod or reel. "Lori, if you need to take a few hours to get some personal stuff done, you can certainly do it. I'm planning to be here and Dick is here as well. Between us, we should be able to deal with anything that comes along."

"That's thoughtful of you, Parker. I do have some errands I've been putting off. Are you sure you'll be okay if I'm gone for a few hours?" Lori Black had begun working for Parker as a part-time sales employee. At that time, she was beginning to study for a Master's degree in fishery science at the University of Montana in Missoula. She was now in the middle of writing her Master's thesis which was focused on whirling disease in trout. She had decided to take a few months off from her writing to work part-time with her mother, Karen Black, in the Black Real Estate Agency in West Yellowstone. The combination of two part-time jobs meant she was working full-time. Subsequent to his moving to West Yellowstone and meeting with Karen during the purchase of his home on Duck Creek, Karen and he had developed a relationship which, at one time, looked as if it would blossom into a substantial one. For whatever reason, Parker hadn't felt any significant attraction and concluded that while Karen would be a good friend, anything more than friendship wasn't in the cards. Every so often, Karen would attempt to ignite a relationship beyond friendship, but Parker never reciprocated.

"I'm sure," replied Parker. "I'm caught up stocking flies. I can be available for any customer if necessary. Dick will be finished soon checking the rods and reels so he's also available for customers. You go." Thanking him for being considerate, Lori left the shop leaving Dick and Parker to take care of whatever might occur. Three customers did spend time in the shop and Parker was able to help them make the correct purchases for their particular fishing needs, including a pair of waders and a wading staff. After about an hour, Parker's phone chirped indicating a text had arrived. Checking the sender, Parker saw it was from Beth. *Is Gretchen there?* Parker replied with his own text. *No, she didn't come in today.* Following what seemed to be no more than a few seconds, his phone rang. Glancing at the number, he recognized it immediately. "Hi, Beth. I just sent you a reply to your text."

"I got it. That's why I'm calling. I've been trying to contact Gretchen all morning. I've texted and called, leaving messages. No response from her. Do you have any idea where she might be?"

"As far as I know, she's at their cabin. She called me last night asking if it was okay if she didn't come in today. She said she didn't have any clients to guide. She also said Liz was coming to the cabin and had something special to show her. Now you know what I know."

"It's unusual for her to not return my calls or respond to my texts," replied Beth. "I suppose I shouldn't be concerned. She is a big girl and I shouldn't be so possessive. Now that I know she has the day off, she's probably out and about enjoying herself. I'll keep trying to contact her. If you hear from her, please tell her to contact me."

"Will do and I wouldn't worry. As you said, she's a big girl."

"One more thing," said Beth. "Our picnic. I really enjoyed our time together. I have an idea. Since I'm the one who brought you your wonderful woman fly fishing guide, I think I should be rewarded with a dinner at the Firehole River Ranch. And I don't want to wait very long. What do you say?"

"You knew what my answer would be before you asked, didn't you? Your company for dinner at the Firehole River Ranch would be my pleasure. How about we meet there tomorrow evening at 6:30 p.m.?"

"Tomorrow evening, 6:30 p.m. See you then and there. If you hear from Gretchen, please let me know right away."

CABIN 17, LOWER VILLAGE, GRANT VILLAGE, YELLOWSTONE NATIONAL PARK, WYOMING

She closed her laptop computer after entering all the information and data she had compiled from her visit with Marsha Sanders-VanderWiele. Marsha was twenty-five percent Crow and a fifth generation descendant of Spotted Deer, the daughter of Running Bear and his widow, who had lived in Swift Eagle's village and known John Colter. Marsha had verified some of the information Liz had obtained from Bev Conner. She also said she didn't know anything about the majority of information Liz mentioned. There was something about how Marsha had answered Liz which suggested to Liz that Marsha wasn't totally forthcoming. Liz had the feeling Marsha was holding back and not telling her everything she knew about the relationships among Swift Eagle, John Colter, and Spotted Deer. Even though Liz felt Marsha wasn't totally forthcoming, she had said something which had caused Liz to become very excited. Marsha told her some old materials, which had been passed down to her mother from her grandmother, who had received them from her grandmother, were located in the basement of the Crow History Museum, at least that is where Marsha assumed they were located. She had given the materials to the Museum and had placed them in the basement herself so unless someone else had moved them, the materials should still be there. Marsha said she never had bothered to look through the materials herself. She had stated quite vehemently with some disdain that she had no interest in old, worthless stuff.

Upon completing her interview with Marsha, Liz had driven from Livingston directly to Crow Agency and the Museum. Gaining access to the basement of the Museum, she had combed through all the material in various files, boxes, and drawers of old storage cabinets. It had been a time consuming process and several times she wondered if Marsha had been mistaken or if the materials had been removed. She kept at it and her perseverance paid off. She located materials in a drawer of an old storage cabinet which was wedged behind several boxes. The boxes had been placed on top of each other, essentially hiding the cabinet from view. She didn't know if these materials were among those which Marsha said she had placed there but it didn't make any difference to Liz. It was what was contained among the materials that mattered, not how they had found their way to the basement of the Museum.

Sure enough, among the materials were several items related to Swift Eagle, his village, Spotted Deer and her mother, and John Colter. She used her phone camera to take photos and then sent them to her own e-mail address. Among the materials were pieces of birch bark with what appeared to be sketches that seemed to be a map of sorts. She took several photos of the bark using different lighting so the sketches would be as clear as possible. Marsha hadn't said anything about birch bark. *I wonder if Marsha knew about the bark and chose not to tell me. Maybe she was hoping I wouldn't find the materials at all. Maybe the bark came from another source and wasn't part of the materials Marsha knew about. Perhaps I simply got lucky.* Sitting back she closed her eyes. For what must have been the twentieth time, at least it felt like she had interpreted the meaning of the sketches that many times, she thought about a particular sketch. It was on a yellowed piece of birch tree bark which seemed to her to be different than the others. She had spent hours trying to understand what this one particular sketch conveyed. She had found the piece of bark at the bottom of a pile of old documents in a drawer of the cabinet. It was anyone's guess how long the piece of bark had been in the drawer. From the looks of the materials on top of the bark, someone had moved them but hadn't, it appeared, looked beneath them. *Someone must have been in a hurry. Why the piece of bark had gone unnoticed was anyone's guess.* It was sort of a miracle the materials had survived, she thought. The fact they had survived meant the bark had also survived and in fairly good shape, good enough for Liz to be able to distinguish some of the markings in the bark. With her knowledge of how Native Americans used markings and sketches to indicate customs and locations and by putting two and two together, she concluded the markings did indeed constitute a map. She had learned enough from reading the historical documents regarding Swift Eagle to know the folklore about his hiding pieces of rock with gold in them in Yellowstone. Historians assumed the location of the pieces of rock had gone with Swift Eagle to the grave. Taking the lighted magnifying glass and looking again at the markings, Liz felt her heart beat increase. Taking deep breaths, she focused. *It might be, yes, it might be. It might be that what I'm looking at is Swift Eagle's map of the location of the pieces of rock he had hidden.*

Because of the enormous impact the map would have if her conclusion proved true, she also spent hours reviewing her work trying to identify any misinterpretations she may have made. She had tried to keep her emotions at bay as she carefully studied the markings. Her heartbeat had increased and her breathing became more pronounced as she realized the ramifications of what she thought the markings conveyed, assuming her interpretations were accurate. Attempting to project herself back more than two hundred years into the mind of a chief of the Crow Tribe wasn't science but a guessing game. *Perhaps I've got it all wrong. Perhaps it isn't a map at all. Maybe there isn't anything significant at all in the markings. Maybe I have misinterpreted what the person who made these markings wanted to capture or convey. But, what if I am correct? Then what?* She knew, if she was correct in her interpretation of the markings, it would lead to something significant, enormously significant beyond what could be imagined. If Liz had it right, finding and interpreting these markings accurately would be a coup of incredible proportions. It would easily establish her as a major player in the Native American and early western United States' research and academic communities.

She was excited about sharing her discovery with Professor Boersma. Even though her discovery wasn't in her area of research for her dissertation, it would be such an earth shaking discovery that it would certainly add to her being awarded her Ph.D. degree. Then many doors would swing open for her as a woman with a Ph.D. in a field of study and research encompassing the lives of Native Americans in the early western United States. What was done eventually with her discovery, and by whom, were of secondary importance to her. She realized her findings would trigger an enormous investigation and exploration frenzy. With potentially millions, possibly even billions of dollars at stake, it would be a frenzy of incredible proportions. The legal ramifications associated with her discovery, if it was as enormous and significant as she thought and hoped it would turn out to be, were out of her area of expertise. Skilled and knowledgeable lawyers would need to be commissioned to study and investigate what she believed she had discovered. The lawyers would have a financial bonanza, given the complexities and intricacies of her discovery, even if she was only somewhat accurate in her interpretation of the markings.

Her thoughts shifted to Gretchen, who should be arriving shortly. She was grateful Gretchen was living with her and that they had reestablished their friendship. Even though there was one thing about Gretchen which troubled Liz, she trusted her more than she did Professor Boersma and certainly more than Aaron. Thinking of Aaron, she asked herself, *What can I do to get rid of him without hurting his feelings? There isn't any chemistry between us. He keeps bugging me and I simply don't have any interest in having any kind of a relationship with him. Sure, we can be friends, but that's it. I need to make it clear to him there is no future for us. He needs to stick with his tour bus driving and forget about me.* Her thoughts returned to Gretchen. *Can I really trust her? Something is going on with her that bothers me. She has changed since we met. I can't figure out what it is. I probably should ask her about it but not until after I've talked with Professor Boersma.* Before meeting him and showing him the markings on the piece of bark, she wanted to share her excitement about her findings with someone outside the academic community. *I'd prefer someone totally neutral and objective, but finding someone like that would take time and I'm anxious to move forward. Gretchen's aunt Beth might be someone I could contact but she is so busy in her position with Yellowstone. I should just stick with Gretchen although there is something going on with her that isn't right.* She was the only person who came to mind who would enable Liz to move forward quickly. Liz just wasn't sure about Professor Boersma. He could be difficult and when he realized there might be money associated with her discovery, all bets about his seeing her through the final portion of the process of earning her Ph.D. would be off. *Given his track record, he must be scrambling to find sources of funding, probably writing grant proposals. He doesn't enjoy writing and he isn't good at it either. In fact, he'd avoid doing it if he didn't need the money. If he could get his hands on money without doing any work, he'd certainly go for it. Maybe this is the motivation behind his new found interest in my research. Normally, I'd have to go to his office at the university to discuss my research. Now, he's coming here. Something happened to change his interest level. I'll have to be alert to whatever it might be.*

Gretchen had been her roommate in college for a couple of years before their individual choice of a college major, followed by life after college, had resulted in their pursuing their own interests and drifting apart. They had recently connected via Facebook and when Gretchen had posted her volunteer status with her father's cousin, who was the Assistant Superintendent of Yellowstone, Liz had gone to Mammoth to meet Gretchen and they had reconnected. When Gretchen had become a fly fishing guide with a fly fishing shop in West Yellowstone, the Assistant Superintendent had used her status within Yellowstone to obtain a cabin in Grant Village to provide housing for Gretchen since the distance from where Gretchen would be living in Grant Village to West Yellowstone was considerably less than from Mammoth. They had used their Facebook posts to become roommates again. Gretchen was shocked when Liz had said she would cover all their living expenses since the cabin had been provided through Gretchen's aunt Beth. Liz knew Gretchen had very little money and one of the things that bothered her was Gretchen's continual talking about getting rich. The fly fishing guide job had been a Godsend for Gretchen. It brought her enough money to cover her costs of commuting back and forth to West Yellowstone. Liz knew Gretchen was constantly thinking of ways to obtain more money. Gretchen was proud and Liz didn't think she would accept money from her, either as a gift or a loan. Maybe Liz would broach the subject when the time seemed more appropriate to do so.

Gretchen had earlier sent Liz a text telling her she was on her way to the cabin. She was eager to learn the exciting news which Liz wanted to share with her. Liz had texted back and said she too was excited. She added that her dissertation professor was coming to the cabin and they would have to wait awhile before he arrived. Gretchen had texted back to tell Liz she was passing Old Faithful and would arrive at the cabin in about one-half hour.

TRAVELING BETWEEN FISHING BRIDGE AND GRANT VILLAGE, YELLOWSTONE NATIONAL PARK, WYOMING

His car was on its last legs. He had been nursing it for the past few months hoping to avoid having to spend money, which he didn't have, to keep it going. It was nearing 200,000 miles and even though he knew some Subaru owners had driven their cars for more than that, he didn't want to push his luck. He needed a dependable car for his forthcoming exit from Yellowstone. Having the money to purchase one was a motivating factor behind his going to see Liz today to implement his plan to get money from her. He had developed his plan for approaching her, gaining her trust, and acquiring the money in the form of a loan from her which, of course, he never planned to pay back. Acquiring the loan was the tricky part. He was counting on his persuasive powers, compelling personality, and knowing the right buttons to push to gain her trust. If she refused to loan him the money, he would be forced to take it. *If I have to, I'll take the money. I'll threaten her. I'll use force if I have to. I know she keeps at least $10,000 in cash in her cabin. She told me she did. Not smart of her to keep that much cash on hand, but it surely is good for me. If she is dumb enough to have more than $10,000 laying around, I'll get that too.*

Looking at the passenger seat, he saw the handgun. He didn't like guns. He didn't own one. Never had. His father had insisted he learn the correct way to handle a gun and how to shoot it. He had convinced himself he might need one to persuade Liz to loan him the money. He simply had to take the gloves off. No pussy-footing around. He had taken the handgun from the locker at the Canyon Ranger Station the night before. He learned from Betsy Slager, a seasonal information assistant at the Ranger Station, about a master key for the locks in the Station. She had also provided other information which would help him find his way around the Station. A few drinks together and some flirting with hints of future amorous activities had loosened her tongue about the key, where to find it, and how best to get into the Station. He waited until after midnight to enter the Station through a window which Betsy had told him wasn't locked at night. Why the window wasn't locked he didn't know and didn't care. Seemed irresponsible to him but he was glad it wasn't locked. An overcast night, with no moonlight to speak of, also was fortunate for him. He had been careful to wear latex gloves to avoid his fingerprints being left on any surface. He wore dark clothing and used a ski mask so only his eyes weren't covered. Thanks, again, to Betsy, he knew there were no security cameras or motion sensing lights to announce or record his breaking and entering. Using the key to open a locker Betsy described to him, he found the handgun. With any luck, it wouldn't be missed for another day or two, more than enough time to accomplish his plan and leave Yellowstone. He would drop the handgun into a thermal feature, never to be found. There was no way the theft of the handgun could be traced to him since it would disappear forever. He had first worried about Betsy blabbing to someone. However, after thinking about it for awhile, he was confident she would keep her mouth shut. If she blabbed, it would implicate her. No, he wasn't concerned about Betsy.

As he drove into Grant Village, his mobile phone rang. Glancing at the screen, he saw the call was from his employer, the Yellowstone Yellow Bus Tour Company. *What do they want? I told them I was sick.* He toyed with answering it but decided against it, allowing the call to go to messaging. He listened to it. *Aaron, I know you're sick but I'm wondering if you are well enough to come in and give us a couple of hours. We're backed up with customers. We have a bus available but no driver. Give me a call back as soon as you can.* Aaron smiled as he thought about the surprise and frustration his Yellow Bus employer was soon going to experience when he never again showed up for work. He told himself to forget about those buses and his driving job. He certainly wouldn't miss the ignorant tourists with their stupid questions. *I'm moving on. Liz is my meal ticket. Her money is going to make good things happen for me.*

He found the location of Cabin 17 on the map of Grant Village in the lodging information kiosk. Driving along the gravel road toward the cabin, he again looked at the handgun on the passenger seat. *I really hope I don't have to use it but I will if I have to. If she refuses to give me a loan, when she sees the gun, she'll know I mean business. I need that money. Pure and simple.* Spotting Cabin 17, he saw a Honda CRV parked near it. *If I remember correctly, Liz told me the woman living with her uses her aunt's SUV. I think Liz told me she was a former college roommate. I hope there aren't other people here. Her roommate's presence is already a problem and more people would only make it worse. I haven't come this far to back away now. I'll have to deal with whatever I find.* Taking the handgun, he placed it into the pocket of his jacket and walked toward the door of the cabin.

CROW RESERVATION, CROW AGENCY, MONTANA

Elizabeth Buikema was a problem. Her inquisitiveness could quickly become a disaster if allowed to continue. Bryson had learned enough from her Facebook page and Twitter postings to conclude he had to derail her from going any further in investigating Swift Eagle's actions. It never ceased to amaze him what some people entered into their Facebook page. Elizabeth Buikema was one such person. He had found what he needed to know in order to confront her from her postings. He had decided he needed to confront her and ultimately stop her. She had described the cabin in Grant Village in Yellowstone where she was living with a former college roommate. He was on his way there now. He hoped she would be alone when he arrived at her cabin. He needed to be alone with her when he confronted her. He would do whatever he needed to do to stop her. She could not be allowed to investigate any further into the life of Swift Eagle. She certainly had to be stopped from investigating where Swift Eagle may have hidden his pieces of rock. If there were pieces of rock with gold in them and if Swift Eagle had hidden them, they belonged to the Crow Tribe, not to this white woman, the federal government, or anyone else who might find them. Even if Yellowstone was now Federal land, it was Crow land when Swift Eagle and his village existed. The Feds had stolen it from the Crows by declaring it a national park with no input from his people. He was going to do something about that violation of his people's heritage. If there was gold in the rocks, they belonged to the Crow Tribe, period. He would make sure of it.

He and his team had carefully reviewed whatever they could get their hands on from the sparse records of the Crow Tribe. Unfortunately, what records did exist weren't located in any one location. Over the years, no group or individual had devoted the time and energy necessary to bring together, in one location, historical records and documents of the Crow Tribe. The history of the Tribe was scattered across the Crow Reservation. It was one thing if family members had kept and organized historical materials which had been handed down from one generation to the next. It was an entirely different matter if a generation didn't care and whatever historical documents had been handed down were essentially forgotten and either discarded or placed who knew where. It was this latter situation which had occupied the overwhelming majority of the team's time and energy. The frustration dealing with the disorganization was too often discouraging and overwhelming.

After a long period of time during which nothing significant had been found about the Tribe's ancestors, a break had occurred. Bryson viewed the break as the ancestors rewarding him for his diligence in wanting to honor their lives. What he had discovered was what today might be called a diary. It had been written by a teenage Crow girl named Willow Bird Song. He had found it in the bottom of a box in a storage unit which the Bird Song family used for storing household belongings. They had used the unit very sporadically. David Bird Song had told Bryson the storage unit was really used to get stuff out of sight and out of mind. When Bryson saw the box, he wasn't going to give it any attention but he felt someone whispering in his ear telling him to open it and see what it contained. Looking back, he believed it was the ancestors telling him to not neglect the box.

He had found Willow Bird Song's diary among the folds of a blanket which served as a type of wrapping. That it was wrapped so tightly in a woven banket and enclosed in a box served to preserve it well enough so that the writing was still legible. At the time, Bryson had wondered if he would violate some sacred bond with the ancestors if he read Willow Bird Song's writings. He convinced himself it would be okay as long as anything personal about her stayed personal and he would keep anything personal about Willow to himself. Much of her writings were about situations she dealt with as a teenager. Occasionally, she would write about a conversation with her grandmother. Bryson had almost decided to forgo reading more of the diary when he read about a conversation between Willow and her grandmother during which her grandmother talked about pieces of rock with gold in them which Chief Swift Eagle had hidden. Furthermore, according to the diary, Swift Eagle had told a white man about the pieces of rock and given him a map of their hidden location. In turn, this white man had shared the map with the daughter of Running Bear, a warrior in Swift Eagle's village who had been killed by the Blackfoot.

Willow Bird Song's diary had given new life to Bryson's investigation. His purpose was now crystal clear. He must find Swift Eagle's pieces of rock before anyone else and claim them for the Crow Tribe. The gold in them would have a dramatic and positive impact on the Crow Tribe. His people had been isolated, put down, and forgotten for much too long. Broken promises and neglect had been their existence. He could change all that. He could bring positive and meaningful change for his people and, in so doing, honor the ancestors. Swift Eagle's pieces of rock meant new life for his people. Grandmother Conner had told him about her conversation with Elizabeth Buikema. Somehow, she had learned about Swift Eagle and Running Bear's daughter. If she hadn't yet learned about the hidden location of the pieces of rock, she soon might. That would be a disaster. He couldn't allow that to happen. The ancestors were counting on him. His people were counting on him. The ancestors had told him to research Willow Bird Song's diary. They and his current fellow tribe members expected him to be a warrior and protect the Tribe. Elizabeth Buikema and anyone else she might have told about Swift Eagle's pieces of rock couldn't be allowed to continue their investigations. *No one is going to cheat my people out of what is rightfully theirs. I'm going to be the reincarnation of Swift Eagle. I'm going to find and claim his gold. Nothing will stop me. I'll be a warrior. If I must, I'll kill anyone who tries to take what is rightfully theirs from my people.*

Entering Grant Village, he looked on the lodging information kiosk for the location of Cabin 17. The map showed that it was at the end of a gravel road and separated from other cabins. As he drove slowly toward Cabin 17, he recognized Elizabeth Buikema's pickup. He had seen pictures of it on her Facebook page. Another car and a SUV parked by Cabin 17 probably meant that two or more people were with her. *Too many people for me to confront her. I need to confront her when she and I are alone. I can hang around and wait until whoever is with her leaves but that might not happen for quite some time. I have other places I need to be.* As he continued to watch the cabin, a plan emerged. Opening the console, he took out the gps tracker he always carried with him. Walking slowly from tree to tree and looking to see if anyone was watching him, he made his way to Elizabeth Buikema's pickup. Activating the tracker, he placed it under the rear bumper. He made his way back to his pickup and waited a few minutes to see if anyone came out of the trees who might have seen him. Satisfied that no one had, he checked the receiver to make sure it was receiving the signals from the tracker. A blinking red dot on the screen showed the location of Elizabeth Buikem's pickup at the end of a road in the Lower Village of Grant Village. Confident he would be able to follow and locate Elizabeth Buikema's pickup, it was only a matter of time and he would be able to confront her. Starting his pickup, he drove away from Cabin 17.

Driving past Yellowstone Lake on his way back to the reservation, he realized he could make Elizabeth Buikema come to the reservation where he could confront her. Pulling to the side of the road, he took his mobile phone and called Grandma Conner. After three rings, she answered. He explained what he wanted her to do. She said she would call Elizabeth, as soon as they finished talking. and tell her she had remembered more about Swift Eagle and if Elizabeth wanted to know about what she remembered, she should come as soon as possible. Thanking Grandma Conner, he ended the call . *Perfect. I will be able to confront Elizabeth at the nursing home and stop her from doing anymore snooping.*

TRAVELING THE HIGHWAY BETWEEN THE SOUTH ENTRANCE AND GRANT VILLAGE YELLOWSTONE NATIONAL PARK, WYOMING

He wondered if this trip to learn from Liz what she felt so excited about would be a colossal waste of time. *What can be so important for her to be so excited? It's unusual for her to act this way. Very outside her character. Maybe it really is something momentous. Probably not. She's probably all worked up over nothing. What if I'm wrong? What if she's made a significant discovery? She sure was acting that way during our conversation. In case she has discovered something big, I need to know what it is. There might be money to be had. I can certainly use every free dollar I can find. I can't overlook any possible source of funds, no matter how remote the possibility. I'll find out soon enough what this is all about. Let's hope this doesn't end up to be a wild goose chase.*

As he drove along the shore of Lewis Lake, he found himself fantasizing about the possibility Liz had made a historical discovery. If she had, he could use it to turn upside down the academic world of so-called scholars devoted to researching the early explorers of the western United States and the lives of Native Americans during the time of the explorers. She told him she had discovered evidence of John

Colter living in a Crow village. What he found most interesting was that Colter had been told by a Crow chief named Swift Eagle about the existence of pieces of rock which, rumor had, contained gold. Colter, in turn, before his death, had apparently told a Crow squaw about the pieces of rock and their hidden location. Most importantly, the Crow chief had made a sketch, on a piece of birch bark, which showed the location of the pieces of rock. Liz claimed the piece of birch bark was in her possession. Hearing about the possibility of undiscovered gold triggered an instant interest on Harold's part. Thoughts of what he could do with the money derived from the gold became active in his mind shortly after Liz told him about what she had discovered. He saw his future unfolding before him. Gold meant money. Unlimited money. So much money he would be able to do what he wanted, when he wanted, where he wanted, and with whom he wanted. He would never again have to scrounge for funds.

If Liz was accurate in her assessment of what she had discovered, he realized he needed to find a way to move her aside so he could claim the discovery for himself. When she had contacted him and told him about her discovery, he had used the strongest words he could muster to direct her not to let anyone else know about her discovery or his coming to meet her at her cabin. He didn't want anyone else near that piece of birch bark before he had been able to review it. He needed to see it for himself. He had threatened to make her life miserable to the point of withholding his approval of her dissertation if she told anyone else about her discovery. *Sorry, Liz, I need it more than you. If it's a truly historic discovery, it's going to be mine no matter what I have to do to get it.*

Turning into the entrance to Grant Village, a pickup drove past. *Was that Liz driving? It looked like her but I'm not sure. If it was her, why would she be leaving? She told me she would be waiting for me. I sure hope I haven't made this trip for nothing. If she isn't at her cabin, she's going to hear about it.* He checked the lodging information kiosk which showed the location of every cabin. Cabin 17 was located in the far back corner of Lower Village and set apart from other cabins. Looking toward it, he saw two vehicles parked near it. One was a Honda CR-V and the other an old Subaru. His anger rose. *Where is Liz' pickup? Was it the one that drove past me? Why are these vehicles here? There must be some other people here. Probably more than one person. Is Liz even here? I told her not to tell anyone about her discovery or my coming. This is really going to complicate matters.*

OFFICE OF THE ASSISTANT SUPERINTENDENT, ADMINISTRATION BUILDING, HEADQUARTERS, YELLOWSTONE NATIONAL PARK, MAMMOTH, MONTANA

Now she was concerned; no, worried big time was more accurate. She had sent two texts and called twice, leaving two voice messages. Gretchen had not responded to any of them. Thinking Gretchen might be in an area where there was no mobile phone service network, she decided to try and reach Liz. Calling Liz's phone, she left a voice message. She also sent Liz a text. Same result as with Gretchen. No response. She had checked both their Facebook pages. Nothing about where either had gone. No mention of their plans. Filled with worry, she said to herself, "*Something's wrong. I can feel it in my gut. It certainly isn't a coincidence they are both not communicating at the same time. Both wouldn't have dropped all communication at the same time unless they are together somewhere in the backcountry with no service. Gretchen should have told me about her plans. I don't like this, not at all. Something is terribly wrong. I just know it.*" Taking a couple of deep breaths to calm herself, she buzzed her administrative assistant. "Yes, what's up?"

"Larry, please find out who the closest ranger or security person is to Grant Village. Once you know, have that person contacted and told to call me immediately. No e-mail or text. I want a call directly to me. When whoever it is calls, don't hesitate to let me know immediately, regardless of where I am or what I'm doing. I must talk with the person. It's important."

"I'll get on it right away."

As soon as she finished talking with Larry, Beth called Parker. After four rings, his answering message clicked on. *"You've reached Parker Williams, owner of the Gold Medal Fly Fishing Shop. Please leave your message. I'll return your call as soon as I can. You can also call the shop to talk with any of us. Enjoy your day."* "Parker, it's Beth. I'm worried sick. I haven't heard from Gretchen. I also tried contacting Liz. No contact with her either. Please call me as soon as you can." Ending the call, she said to herself, *"What else should I do? What can I do? It's irresponsible of them to go into the backcountry without telling anyone. Wait a minute. Get a hold of yourself. Think. Our newly computerized data base will tell me where they are. Stupid me."* Swiveling her chair around to face her computer on the table behind her desk, she logged into the BackCountry Permit and Camping Data Base. It listed every overnight backcountry hiking or camping permit issued in Yellowstone over the prior two weeks. Information about the person to whom the permit was issued, driver's license or passport number of the person, number of people in the party, planned destination of the party, age of each person, duration of time planned to be in the backcountry, trails to be used, campsite assigned by Yellowstone, permit number, and other data were all available. Scrolling through the data, Beth found no record of a permit issued to either Gretchen or Liz. *Could they have been so stupid not to take out a permit? They know the rules. No one is above the rules when it comes to being in Yellowstone's backcountry. I'm going to have it out with both of them when I talk with them.* She knew every year some visitors to Yellowstone would venture into the backcountry to camp without obtaining a permit. The permit was not meant to restrict them from enjoying the grandeur of Yellowstone by going into the backcountry and getting away from the crowds of visitors. Statistics related to where visitors went in Yellowstone showed nearly eighty-five percent never ventured further from a road by more than twenty-five yards. Permits were required as a safety measure for those visitors who did venture away from the roads and crowds. If something happened–sprained ankle, broken leg or arm, debilitating sickness, heart attack, encounter with wildlife resulting in injury, burns from being too close to thermal features–whatever the situation, the rescue personnel of Yellowstone had to knew where to go to locate the visitor. The visitor's location was much easier to determine based on the information provided by the visitor when obtaining a permit. Without the information included in the permit, injured visitors calling 911 and saying they were in the backcountry somewhere in the vicinity of the Grand Canyon of the Yellowstone River, for example, didn't cut it in terms of providing rescue personnel with the information they needed to locate the visitor. Yellowstone comprised more square miles than Rhode Island or Delaware and it was crisscrossed by hundreds of trails. Even with satellite technology, it sometimes took more than twenty-four hours for rescue personnel or park rangers to locate an injured visitor if the visitor hadn't been issued a permit. On a few occasions, rescuers arrived too late, especially if hypothermia occurred. With elevations of 9,000 plus feet above sea level throughout Yellowstone, overnight temperatures could plunge, even in the summer, causing excessive hypothermia and even death.

Her heartbeat increased as her feelings of anxiety increased. *Come on, someone call me. Where are people when you really need them? Call me! Hanging around here is driving me crazy. Where are those two? If they went into the backcountry, why didn't they obtain a permit? Why didn't Gretchen tell me her plans?* Her thoughts were interrupted by the buzz of her intercom. "Yes, Larry."

"I have Marlene VanderBrink on line one. She's the security person closest to Grant Village."

"Thanks, Larry." Pushing the line one button on her desk phone, she said, "Marlene, this is Beth Richardson. Have I interrupted something important?"

"No, Assistant Superintendent Richardson, I'm not into anything pressing, but I must admit I'm somewhat nervous. We've never met, I don't believe, let alone talked, and you are the Assistant Superintendent. Have I done something wrong? Am I in trouble?"

"I apologize for us not meeting, Marlene. My fault. I'd like to think I have met all our full-time staff, but that's obviously not the case. I'll make it a point to meet you soon. You don't need to be nervous at all. You've done nothing wrong. I assure you. Each of us here at Yellowstone has a role to play and mine isn't any more important than yours; just different. Please, don't be nervous or anxious."

"Thanks for saying that," replied Marlene. "I'm sure you have a whole lot of important matters on your plate. When my boss contacted me, he said it was important I contact you right away. I hope I'm not tardy."

Laughing, Beth responded, "Tardy. I haven't heard that word since elementary school. I was tardy all the time. No, you aren't tardy and yes, it's important. I must tell you I am going to ask you for a personal favor. It has nothing to do with your job or mine. I normally don't have staff do personal things for me. I don't believe in it and it isn't good policy or practice. But I'm in a bind. Simply put, I've no other way to accomplish what is important to accomplish."

"If I can be bold, Assistant Superintendent Richardson, you sound nervous and frustrated. It's none of my business but I don't like the sound of your voice. I can tell something is bothering you. If I can help you, I'm ready to do so. If you're okay with me helping with something personal for you, I'm okay with it too."

"Thanks for understanding, Marlene. Yes, I'm anxious. Knowing you're available and willing to help me, I'm no longer frustrated. My anxiety won't be eliminated until I know for sure what I'm going to ask you to find out for me. Marlene, this may turn out to be a big nothing. I hope it is a big nothing. Here's what I need you to do. I need you to go to Grant Village and check Cabin 17 in Lower Village. One of my employees and her woman friend live there. I've tried to contact both of them individually for quite a while now and received no response. Texts, e-mails, and calls to their phones have resulted in no response. Nothing on their Facebook pages either. You can probably understand why I'm concerned. If you would please check the cabin, maybe they are there.

If they are, I don't know why they haven't responded to me but I'll deal with that later. If they are there, please ask them to contact me. If they aren't there, see if you can locate something indicating where they may be or where they might have been going."

"I can certainly do that for you," replied Marlene. What about entering the cabin? I won't have a search warrant. I don't want to get in trouble for breaking and entering."

"Marlene, I appreciate your honesty and your wanting to avoid trouble. I wouldn't ask you to do this if I had the slightest thought I was placing you at risk. This is against my operational policy and how I act, but this is one time I'm going to violate my own policy. I'm also going to pull rank. As you are probably aware, Director Terpstra reports to me. After we finish this call, I'm going to contact him and tell him what I directed you to do. All will be well for you, trust me."

"Everything people say about you, Assistant Superintendent Richardson, is you are honest, a straight shooter, and stick up for your people. Your word is good enough for me. I'll be on my way to Grant Village immediately. I'll call you as soon as I learn something."

"I'm glad to hear you've been told those things about me. I do try as I know you do too. One more thing, Marlene. From now on it's Beth, not Assistant Superintendent Richardson, okay?"

"Sure enough, Beth. I can't disagree with my superior."

"Forget the superior stuff too, Marlene. Thanks again. Yes, please contact me as soon as you know something, even if you don't find anything useful."

Ending the call, Beth immediately called Bruce Terpstra. Bruce was Director of Security Services for Yellowstone. She told him about Marlene VanderBrink and what Beth had asked her to do. Bruce assured Beth there would be no report made should Marlene be seen entering Cabin 17. Thanking Bruce for his understanding, she turned to the stack of papers awaiting her attention. *Nothing more for me to do now but wait. I hate having no information.*

PEACEFUL WATERS NURSING HOME, CROW RESERVATION, CROW AGENCY, MONTANA

Bryson parked in the parking lot of the nursing home where he could see every vehicle entering the lot. He waited for Elizabeth Buikema to arrive. He would wait for her to enter the nursing home and be with Grandmother Conner. He had called her again as he was driving to tell her he would be coming to her room while Elizabeth was with her. She hadn't asked why Bryson wanted to meet Elizabeth nor did he tell her. He recognized Elizabeth's pickup as it parked a few parking spaces from the entrance. A woman got out of the driver's side and walked into the nursing home. *I'll give her a few minutes to get to Grandmother Conner's room. Then I'll confront her there. It'll be good to do it in front of Grandma Conner so she can see I'm a warrior standing for our people.*

CABIN 17, LOWER VILLAGE, GRANT VILLAGE, YELLOWSTONE NATIONAL PARK, WYOMING

Marlene VanderBrink had been nervous ever since being told by Director Terpstra she should immediately call Assistant Superintendent Richardson. Director Terpstra had added to her nervousness by emphasizing she should do so immediately. It was important she do so without delay. She couldn't remember doing anything so wrong which would result in the Assistant Superintendent becoming involved with whatever she had done. She had thought she was going to lose her job. She couldn't think of any other reason Assistant Superintendent Richardson would want to talk with her. Thank goodness, that wasn't the reason behind the request. Although Beth had assured Marlene she wouldn't get in trouble, when she entered the cabin without the approval of its occupants or without a legitimate search warrant, her nervousness and anxiety levels remained high. *I'm not comfortable at all with any of this. Can't Beth wait a little longer to hear from her woman friend? It hasn't been that long. At least wait a few more hours.* She really didn't like the situation Beth had placed her in but what do you do when your boss' boss asks you, in a very personal manner as well, to do something? *If I told Beth I wouldn't do it, I may have lost my job. I know people say Beth is fair and not vindictive, but I couldn't risk her possibly being vindictive. That's all water over the dam now anyway. I'm here, so I'd better do what I came to do and get it over with.*

The scene before her struck her as odd. Beth had told her neither of the women living in Cabin 17 had responded to calls, texts, or e-mails from her. Beth believed both had gone somewhere, most likely to an area of Yellowstone where a mobile phone connection was non-existent or spotty at best. One reason some Yellowstone officials carried a satellite phone whenever they went into the backcountry was they always had a connection. If neither of the women were here, why would there be three vehicles parked next to the cabin? *Whose vehicles are these? This tells me Beth's employee is most likely here, as well as some other people too.* She realized she should have asked Beth for more information before coming here. *Do any of these vehicles belong to Beth's employee? I think Gretchen is her name. Should I call Beth and ask her if she knows the vehicle Gretchen drives? What about the other vehicles? What if Beth isn't available right now to talk with me? Do I just wait around here until I hear from her? I need to demonstrate competence to Beth otherwise she might question my ability as a security officer. Beth's employee must be here, given there are three vehicles. Probably the woman she lives with is here too. They are probably enjoying some time with friends and haven't paid attention to any texts or phone calls. What difference does it make anyway whose vehicles these are? I need to determine if Beth's employee is here or if she isn't, try to determine where she might be. That's it. I don't need to know anything about the vehicles or, for that matter, any other people. I need to get on with it.*

Walking toward the front door of the cabin, she wished she had a handgun, just in case something unexpected awaited her. As a security officer, she wasn't issued one. Only full-time rangers, with appropriate training, were issued handguns. The Yellowstone administration didn't want to alarm tourists with too many handguns being visible. Visitors expected rangers to have them but not other Yellowstone employees. The policy made sense, she felt, but in an unknown situation, like the one she was facing, she would feel less vulnerable if she did have a handgun.

Stepping onto the small porch and walking to the door, she raised her hand to knock on the door to announce her presence. Instead, the door opened, catching her off guard and completely by surprise. Pointed at her was a handgun. Before she could comprehend what was happening, she heard the word "sorry". The last thing she heard was an explosion, simultaneously with a searing pain in her chest as everything went blank and dark.

OFFICE OF THE ASSISTANT SUPERINTENDENT, ADMINISTRATION BUILDING, HEADQUARTERS, YELLOWSTONE NATIONAL PARK, MAMMOTH, MONTANA

Her intercom buzzed. Pushing the button to engage it, she said, "Yes, Larry."

"It's Director Terpstra. He says it's an emergency. Line two."

Her heart skipped a beat. *I knew it. Something bad has happened to Gretchen. Marlene hasn't contacted me yet. She must have contacted Bruce instead. Marlene didn't want to tell me. This is going to be very bad.* Steeling herself against what she expected to hear, she punched the line two button and said, "Bruce, Larry said you have an emergency. It's about Gretchen, isn't it?"

"No, Beth, it's not about Gretchen. It's about Marlene VanderBrink. She's been shot. Outside Cabin 17 at Grant Village. That's the cabin where your employee is living. Marlene is on...'"

"Shot! What do you mean shot? What happened?

"As I was saying, Marlene is on her way to Deaconess hospital in Bozeman as we speak. It's going to be touch and go. We're helicoptering her to Deaconess after doing our best to stabilize her and slow the bleeding. She's in excellent condition, which works in her favor, but the blood loss might be too great. We just don't know. Thank goodness Deaconess is a trauma one hospital."

"Who shot her? Why was she shot? Have you arrested the shooter?"

"No, we have no idea who the shooter may be. We don't know much at all about anything that happened. We are working on it. We've contacted the FBI and asked for assistance. Our priority until only a few minutes ago was Marlene. If she pulls through, she will be in intensive care for some time. I suspect she won't be able to talk for several days. We need to catch a break if we're going to catch whoever did this because Marlene isn't able to tell us anything."

Realizing she was the reason Marlene had gone to Grant Village, Beth felt overcome with guilt and emotion. She also had to find out if Bruce knew anything about Gretchen. "Bruce, you're right. Deaconess gives her a fighting chance. The doctors there are real pros. But, I'm responsible for sending Marlene to Grant Village. I put her in a situation where there was something bad going on. I should have gone myself. I feel terrible. What can I do?"

"Don't blame yourself, Beth. If you had gone instead of Marlene, you probably would have been shot. I'm betting Marlene stumbled onto something and the shooter thought she needed to be silenced. What she stumbled upon is anyone's guess. Instead of blaming yourself, pray for Marlene and for the surgeons. My Deputy Director, Alice Hoogstrate, is on her way to Deaconess as we speak. She will keep us informed. There's really nothing else you or any of us can do."

"Bruce, I know this might sound callous and insensitive, even selfish. I don't mean it to be any of those things but I must ask you. Do you have any information about Gretchen? I take it she wasn't at the cabin."

"As far as we know now, and our information is coming from a visitor who found Marlene after the shooting occurred, no one was at the cabin when this person, a visitor from Nebraska who is staying with her family in Cabin 18, came upon the scene. We may have caught a break, thanks to this visitor. If she hadn't been curious and gone to investigate, Marlene would have bled out."

"So, somebody saw what happened. You have a witness. You said she, so your witness is a woman. Can she provide a description of the shooter? We can have all the entrances to the park blocked so the shooter won't be able to get out of the park. Have you done that yet?"

"It's happening as we speak. We're letting vehicles exit the park but only after carefully checking each vehicle. Not the best public relations for us since visitors are antsy and get angry when they wait in line to exit. But if the shooter is trying to exit the park using a vehicle, we need to check every vehicle that's leaving. Unfortunately, the shooter could abandon the vehicle in some remote place and walk out. That's most likely not the case, but it can't be ruled out."

"What about your witness? Did she see the vehicle the shooter used?"

"I wish she was a witness, but she isn't. Remember what I said. She arrived after Marlene was shot. No one else was around. Most likely there was a five minute or so gap between the shooting and our woman visitor finding Marlene. Enough time for the shooter to get away."

"Okay, I stand corrected. She isn't a witness. But, what does she know?

"Here's what she told us. She heard what she thought was a shot but didn't think anything of it until she heard a vehicle drive very fast by her cabin coming from the direction of Cabin 17. She doesn't know if it was a car, pickup, SUV, or whatever. She thought it strange that a vehicle would be traveling so fast so she went outside her cabin to take a look. Cabin 17 is somewhat separated from the other cabins so we are fortunate she has good eyes. She thought she saw something on the porch of Cabin 17 so she walked toward it. When she got closer, she realized what she saw on the porch was a body. It was Marlene. She thought Marlene might have fallen and hurt herself. This woman is a practical nurse which is another Godsend. She knew what to do to slow the bleeding. She first thought the vehicle driving so fast was someone going to get help. We think it was probably the shooter getting away. When the woman saw the blood, she knew something bad had happened. Thankfully, she didn't panic. After she stopped the bleeding as best she could, she called 911. She also wrapped her blouse tightly around where Marlene was bleeding the worst. She might have saved Marlene's life, at least I hope so. The EMTs arrived, stabilized Marlene, slowed the bleeding even more, and started IVs. The woman will be interviewed by the FBI once two agents get here. She may remember more then."

"So, no Gretchen, no Liz, no anyone," replied Beth. "Just a vehicle driving fast away from the cabin." Wondering if the vehicle was her CR-V which Gretchen was using, she continued, "What was the make of the vehicle? Did the woman see it?"

"Nope," said Bruce, "she said she heard it but didn't see it. Why do you ask?"

"Gretchen is using my Honda CR-V. I wondered if it was the vehicle the woman heard."

"It couldn't be. A CR-V is parked by Cabin 17 as we speak. It has a Yellowstone National Park employee sticker. I haven't looked up the number yet to determine who the employee is but now I don't need to. I assume it's yours. Matter of fact, maybe you can help me. There's another vehicle parked there as well, an old green Subaru. It has South Dakota plates. We've asked the South Dakota Highway Patrol to run the plates for us. We should have the results sooner rather than later. We're having the plates of the CR-V run as well but since we now know it is yours, I'll call off the search.

"I have no idea about the Subaru. Another vehicle must have been there and it must have been the shooter's car which the woman heard. Is that the way you figure it, Bruce?"

"Makes as much sense as anything else right now. I need to find who the owner is of the Subaru. It's my only possible clue right now."

"Yeah, once you know the owner, a clue or two about the identification of the shooter might result."

"Beth, you have a good point. Right now, I want to make sure nothing gets disturbed by any curious onlookers before the FBI arrives. Janet VanKampen said two agents would be coming as soon as possible to investigate the scene. Until they get here, I have to make sure nothing is disturbed."

"Bruce, please let me know anything you learn about Marlene. Also, anything about Gretchen or Liz. Keep me informed." Placing the phone in its holder on her desk, Beth placed her head in her hands. *What have I done? I asked an innocent woman to do something for me. I shouldn't have asked her and now she might die because of me. What was I thinking? I also must find out about Gretchen.*

Reflecting on what Bruce had told her, she remembered he had mentioned Janet VanKampen and the FBI. She was grateful for the involvement of the FBI with all its resources and capabilities, but she wasn't grateful for Janet's involvement. Janet VanKampen was the Special Agent in Charge of the Billings, Montana Office of the FBI. It had jurisdiction over criminal activity conducted in Yellowstone since Yellowstone was a federally controlled property. Due to its workload and limited resources, more often than not, the FBI delegated to Yellowstone Security personnel the investigation of crimes in the federally governed national park. Homicides were a different story. Should Marlene VanderBrink pass away and her death be ruled a homicide, the FBI would not delegate responsibility. Investigating homicides remained with the FBI. Janet VanKampen and her agents would be all over a homicide, meaning Janet and Beth would probably come in contact with each other at some time. It was even more likely since Gretchen might be involved somehow in whatever took place at Cabin 17 that resulted in Marlene's shooting. Janet and Beth didn't see eye to eye. Truth be told, they didn't like each other, not due to anything either had done to the other, but out of jealousy over each of their relationships with Parker. Beth knew Janet had come on to Parker quite aggressively in the past. As far as Beth knew, Parker hadn't responded, at least not yet. Janet had even gone as far as deputizing Parker as a temporary FBI agent during a past case Janet was responsible for in Yellowstone. On the other hand, Janet knew about Beth and Parker's on-again, off-again relationship and Beth sensed Janet's jealousy and resentment of her friendship with Parker. *There's nothing I can do about Janet. If she can help find Gretchen and the person who shot Marlene, I will be grateful. I hope she can do both without fawning all over Parker if he comes in contact with her for whatever reason. Speaking of Parker, I better call him and tell him what has happened.*

OFFICE OF THE FBI, BILLINGS, MONTANA

Just what she didn't need. A possible homicide in Yellowstone. She had her hands full with all the current investigations to say nothing of the Secret Service requests to provide agents to assist in covering the appearances of the presidential candidates throughout her region. Now that the presidential campaigns were in full swing, the candidates were crisscrossing the country. Their appearances were a gigantic pain. With so few electoral votes in Wyoming and Montana, why did they bother to visit these states? Concentrate on Florida, Pennsylvania, Ohio, and Colorado, the so-called swing states. Each had more electoral votes than Wyoming and Montana combined. Better yet, stay in Washington, D.C. and campaign via social media and television. *Now I have to take two agents away from their current investigation and send them to Grant Village to investigate the shooting of a Yellowstone female security employee. Hopefully, the woman won't die. Then I can delegate the investigation to the Yellowstone security people.* Janet had discretion to allow other law enforcement agencies to be the lead agency on certain criminal investigations which the FBI would normally undertake. *Carrie and Alex should have arrived at Grant Village by now. They will have secured the scene and looked it over for evidence and clues about what happened. I'm sure they've developed a plan and strategy for what should be done next. Using the helicopter to get them there quickly has hopefully paid off. I'll text Carrie to learn the latest.*

Carrie DeLange and Alex Ritsema were FBI agents in the Billings Office who worked together as a team. Both had been detectives with mid-sized city police departments prior to being recruited by the Bureau. Carrie had worked in Grand Rapids, Michigan, where she had been involved in several high profile cases involving the smuggling of highly-priced artwork from the Netherlands. Prior to joining the Bureau, Alex had been with the Newark, New Jersey Police Department where he led a special crimes unit focused on human trafficking. Carrie was about 5' 7" with short brown hair, which she usually wore pulled back into a pony tail. She was thin and built like a long distance runner. Alex, on the other hand, was 6' 4", weighed 240 and could bench press more than 300 lbs. He had played middle linebacker in college before tearing his knee, which ended his career. Other agents referred to them as the thin and big couple. They worked well together and had been able to bring to conclusion numerous cases which had floundered under other agents.

Janet had tried to establish as many female-male teams as possible given the absurdity of bogus claims of discrimination by FBI female agents against male agents. Some male agents claimed female agents weren't held to the same standards. They also claimed female agents were being treated with kid gloves and weren't required to perform at levels expected of male agents. In all her years with the Bureau, Janet hadn't experienced discrimination or seen it. There wasn't any discrimination of female agents by male agents as far as she was concerned. *I'm a woman and look where I am. Special Agent in Charge of an office with male agents reporting to me. I was never discriminated against and I never witnessed it against other female agents. I also haven't discriminated against male agents.* She believed the bozos in the Justice Department in Washington D.C. were so intent on being inclusive that sub-quality agents were becoming part of the Bureau at an alarming rate in order to demonstrate inclusiveness to the politicians. Thank goodness Carrie and Alex were exceptions. Both were outstanding agents. Neither had ever mentioned discrimination. She knew she could count on them doing a thorough and complete investigation of the crime scene in Yellowstone.

DOWN RIVER FROM THE MIDDLE GEYSER BASIN, FIREHOLE RIVER, YELLOWSTONE NATIONAL PARK, WYOMING

He didn't do this often enough. What could be better than this? Standing thigh level in a famous fly fishing river, with a small geyser along the bank shooting steaming water ten feet into the air with a herd of fifteen bison grazing on the near bank. He was ready to cast his olive-colored number 16 elk hair caddis fishing fly to rainbow trout feeding from the surface of the river. As far as he was concerned, this was the epitome of relaxation and enjoyable activity. Nothing could beat it. He knew other people enjoyed different sporting activities as much as he did fly fishing but this was at the top for him. In the Rocky Mountain West, numerous outdoor activities provided people with many opportunities. Downhill and cross country skiing had exploded in popularity during the past several years. Big Sky ski area, about forty miles north of West Yellowstone, was now a major ski and golf resort drawing people from across the country. But for Parker, fly fishing in and around Yellowstone National Park was at the top of the list of enjoyable outdoor activities.

No other place in the lower forty-eight provided the combination of diverse thermal activity, involving some of the largest and most famous geysers and boiling mud pots in the world. Diverse wildlife, including level one predators, more than one thousand species and varieties of birds and waterfowl were resident for most of the year. The largest freshwater lake west of the Mississippi, hundreds of rivers, streams, and creeks with an abundance of fish and aquatic life, and more than fifty waterfalls including the famous Upper and Lower Falls of the Yellowstone River in the Grand Canyon of the Yellowstone were in the park. He, like many other fly fishers, long ago realized catching fish was secondary to the experience of being surrounded by the grandeur and beauty of Yellowstone, unique in its diversity and breadth of wonders.

He had spotted a pod of trout rising to take some insect floating on the surface of the river. The fish were rising with no regularity which suggested no consistent hatching of insects was occurring. It would take precision in his casting to avoid his imitation fly floating on the surface of the water with drag. Drag on the water was the kiss of death to catching trout when they were focused on eating floating insects from the surface of the water. For some reason, known only to fish, they knew an insect-looking thing which floated on the surface of the water with drag was a fly with a hook and was to be avoided at all costs. Many a fly fisher had been skunked because of drag in their presentation of their fly when casting so it would float on the surface of the water. Parker had learned through trial and error how to control drag and correct for it by mending the fishing line before drag occurred. By flipping the line, whenever it appeared drag was about to begin, that possibility was eliminated and kept the fly floating without drag, just like a real insect would float. It was a technique initially taught and then refined through experience. Nothing short of experience worked. There were no shortcuts. It was one of the reasons fly fishers hired guides. Guides not only knew the places to fish, how to spot where fish were located in a river or stream, which fly was best to use in a particular situation and had the best chance of tricking the fish into thinking it was a real insect to eat, but also how to cast a fly so it would float on the surface of the water without causing drag.

Numerous boulders and rocks were scattered throughout this stretch of the Firehole River. Broken water surrounded these boulders and rocks which, Parker knew, provided security for fish from eagles, osprey, and hawks which lingered overhead. They were watching the surface of the water for a telltale sign of a fish ready to rise to the surface to take a insect floating on the water. Their instincts developed and honed over thousands of years, fish knew broken water didn't allow for the keen eyes of predators flying overhead to see them. Parker knew fish tended to congregate in close proximity to any object which caused the water to be broken so he cast his fly a few feet above a boulder or rock allowing it to float drag-free on the surface of the broken water as it surged past the boulder or rock. On his third cast, he felt the familiar strike of a fish taking his fly. For the next several minutes, he and the fish had a standoff. He didn't want to pull too hard as he could pull the hook from the fish's lip. He also didn't want to play the fish for too long so that it became exhausted and couldn't recover once Parker released it. Experience hooking and landing hundreds of fish had taught Parker to feel through his rod when the fish was beginning to tire too much and he needed to quickly bring it to his net and release it. For the next two hours, he moved slowly down the river always testing his footsteps in the water before firmly planting his feet. Too many times he had taken a tumble when he hadn't been careful enough to feel his way along the bottom of the river before stepping forward. Fortunately, he had escaped injury or even death. Every so often, a person fishing in a river with a strong current would drown because they stumbled and fell into the water, their waders filled with water, and they were swept under the surface of the water or over a waterfall. He had learned no fish was worth taking that level of risk when wading in a stream or river with a significant current.

He had caught and released eight rainbow trout when he heard his phone ring. He carried his phone in a waterproof pocket of his fishing vest where he could easily access it. Without first looking to determine who was calling him, he answered, "You've reached Parker Williams."

"Parker, it's Beth. Can you talk for a few minutes?"

"Not very easily. I'm standing in the middle of the Firehole. If you can hang on for a couple of minutes, I'll work my way over to the bank. Otherwise, I'll call you back in a few minutes."

"I'll wait. Take your time. Be careful."

"Okay I'm in a fairly even-bottom section of the river so it shouldn't take me too long to get to the bank. If for some reason we are cut off, I'll call you back."

"I'll hold and wait until you're to the bank. Take your time and be careful."

As he waded toward the nearest bank, he wondered why Beth was calling. He hoped it wasn't to cancel their dinner. It wasn't the easiest thing to find time when they could be together given their individual work schedules and responsibilities. Maybe she just wanted to talk, but that was unlikely. He thought he heard anxiety in her voice. He hoped nothing had happened to upset her. Arriving at the bank, he placed his rod down and stepped from the water. "Beth, I'm on the bank. What's up?"

"I have some terrible news. I need to talk about it with someone who will understand. A woman security officer has been shot and it's all my fault." Before she could continue, Parker interrupted her.

"What do you mean it's your fault? Who's been shot? Why do you think it's your fault?"

"It's a long story. The short version is I asked her to do a personal favor for me, something I shouldn't have done. Because of me, she ended up being shot. She could die. She's at Deaconess and we won't know for several more hours if she is going to make it. If she doesn't make it, I won't be able to live with myself. I would be responsible for her death."

Hearing the anxiety in her voice and her self-incriminating tone, Parker replied, "Where are you now? I want to come and be with you. We can talk about all this together."

"Would you please? It would be so wonderful to have you here. I'm at a loss to know what to do. I could sure use some smart thinking from you. On top of this horrible shooting, I haven't heard yet from Gretchen. Same with Liz. To make matters worse, Gretchen, or I suppose Liz too, may be mixed up in this shooting. I'm worried big time."

"Of course I'll come. Where are you? What do you mean Gretchen or Liz may be mixed up in the shooting. How? What does either one of them have to do with any of this?"

"I'm in my office. I'm going to leave after we end this call. When we are together I'll tell you what I know. I'll head for your shop. By the time you get there from the Firehole, I should be there. Is it okay that I come there?"

Thinking about the fact the shop didn't provide very much confidentiality since it was a retail business with customers coming in and out, Parker replied, "Better than the shop, come to my home. We can talk in private with no interruptions. In case you get there before me, do you remember the code to the door?"

Parker's home was located on Duck Creek, seven miles north of West Yellowstone. It was set back from Duck Creek about fifteen yards with a view of the Spanish Mountain Range. A gravel road from Highway 191 paralleled Duck Creek and led to the house. "It's been awhile since I stopped at your house and had to use the code. Refresh my memory. I'll write it down," she replied.

Speaking slowly, Parker said, "It's three-star-one-three-nine-zero-six-zero-six. Remember, star, not pound."

"Now I remember. With my mind going bonkers right now, I wrote it down. That way I won't forget." He could hear the emotion in her voice as she continued, "Thanks for being willing to meet me. It means a lot. I should be to your place in about forty-five minutes."

Walking along the bank of the Firehole River, he reached the small parking lot at the end of Fountain Flats Drive where he had parked his Toyota Tacoma pickup. He had purchased the pickup from one of the guides who had decided to leave the Yellowstone area to explore Alaska. It was a 2014 model with only 24,000 miles. Parker had jumped at the opportunity to purchase it. It had sufficient towing capacity for large float boats which he used to guide more than two clients on fly fishing trips on the Madison River outside Yellowstone. He didn't take the time to remove his wading shoes and waders before getting in the pickup. He thought about what Beth had told him as he drove along the road paralleling the Firehole River toward Madison Junction. He continued driving along the Madison River heading toward the west entrance to Yellowstone and the town of West Yellowstone. From there it was a straight shot north for seven miles to his home on Duck Creek. All during the drive, his thoughts were focused on Beth and the situation she had described to him. He wasn't sure what it was which prompted Beth to ask the woman employee to do something for her but it was obvious from their conversation she felt guilty about asking her. He could tell Beth was upset by the tone of her voice. She was blaming herself for this woman being shot. Also, what was going on with Gretchen and, for that matter, Liz? Why hadn't either responded to Beth's numerous attempts to reach them? Why did Beth say they might be involved in the shooting of the Yellowstone employee? How could that be? He had talked with Gretchen last evening and she hadn't said anything which would suggest her being involved in something that resulted in a shooting. She had taken the day off from guiding. That was it. Nothing more. Questions with no answers kept swirling around in his mind as he drove into West Yellowstone. *I'm not going to stop at the shop. I can't take the time. Beth needs me more than the shop does. Lori is totally capable of taking care of things and Dick is probably there as well.*

Driving the seven miles from West Yellowstone to his home, he knew, before Beth even told him, that she was going to take this shooting personally. He knew her well enough to know she wasn't about to sit on the sideline while the shooter was at large. In some way, she was going to become involved. It wasn't in her DNA to let something like this shooting and the possibility of Gretchen being involved in it to pass. He knew Beth was also taking it personally thinking Gretchen had purposely avoided responding to her e-mails, texts, and calls. *Why would Gretchen be avoiding Beth? Is there something going on between the two of them I don't know about? Is Gretchen avoiding Beth on purpose? I'm afraid I know what Beth is going to tell me. I know she is going to tell me that she plans to become personally involved in searching for the shooter and also for Gretchen. Should I discourage her? If I do, it won't do any good. She will search anyway. Do I join her? At least give her moral support? Isn't that what good friends do for each other?*

Turning onto his driveway from the gravel road leading to his home, he saw a Yellowstone Chevy Tahoe parked in front of his home. Beth had been provided with a Tahoe for official use so he assumed she had arrived before him and had already gone into his home. He walked the few yards to the front porch where he sat on a bench by the front door so he could remove his wet wading shoes and waders. As he was removing his waders, the front door opened. Looking at Beth, he could see she had been crying. Standing, he reached out, taking her into his arms in a hug. "It's okay, Beth. It'll be okay."

Not letting go of him, she responded in a choking voice, "It's my fault. Bruce called and said the doctors didn't give Marlene much of a chance. If she dies, Parker, I might as well have been the one who pulled the trigger. And Gretchen may have been there and witnessed the whole thing and now she may be with the shooter or have already been harmed."

Releasing her so he could look at her, he replied, "It isn't your fault. It's the shooter's fault. You don't know if Gretchen was there. She could be somewhere in the backcountry of Yellowstone and out of network connection. You can't assume the worst. Let's go sit down. I'll make some tea." Walking slowly into the house with his arm around Beth, he knew the next several minutes were going to be crucial in keeping her from losing her senses. She sat on the sofa in front of the rock fireplace which dominated the east wall from floor to ceiling of the great room. "I'll go heat the water in the Keurig for tea. You have any special kind you prefer?"

"Right now, it doesn't make any difference. You pick what you like. Thanks so much for being with me. It means a whole lot to me."

He noticed her voice had returned to its normal tone. She had gotten control of her emotions and that was a good sign. *I need to keep her from blaming herself. Get her away from thinking the worst. I know she is worried sick about Gretchen.* Placing a tea bag into the cup of hot water, he brought it to her and sat next to her on the sofa. "Driving here, I tried to remember if Gretchen said anything to me when she called me to tell me she wasn't coming in to the shop. I've tried to remember everything she said which might provide a clue to where she might be but I can't recall anything. What about your last conversation with her? What do you remember?"

"I've racked my brain trying to recall anything, anything at all she might have said about her plans," replied Beth. "I've come up blank. If she is in the backcountry and she didn't obtain a permit, she knows to check in occasionally. No, Parker, my gut tells me she isn't in the backcountry. I'm terrified she was in her cabin when Marlene was shot. My fear is the shooter was there with Gretchen. Bruce told me there is a Subaru parked by the cabin along with my CR-V. He also told me the woman who found Marlene heard a car, maybe a pickup, driving very fast from the cabin. Was it the shooter driving away? Was Gretchen in that car with the shooter? Whose car is the Subaru? Since there must have been at least three vehicles, with one driving away after the shooting, was there someone else, in addition to Gretchen and the shooter, in the cabin when Marlene showed up? Liz was spending lots of time on the Crow Reservation with her research. Maybe something about her research upset the Crows and a hothead decided to take it out on Liz and Marlene got in the way. Questions, Parker, too many questions and no answers. While I was waiting for you to come, I made a decision. I'm going to look for Gretchen. I realize I can't help Marlene but I can possibly help Gretchen."

CABIN 17, LOWER VILLAGE, GRANT VILLAGE, YELLOWSTONE NATIONAL PARK, WYOMING

It hadn't taken long to draw some preliminary conclusions about what had taken place outside and in the cabin regarding the shooting of the Yellowstone woman employee. In their capacity as FBI agents, Carrie and Alex had performed many searches of crime scenes involving a shooting. These searches provided them with experience in knowing what items, positions of those items, and the overall condition of the scene were important and which weren't. "I feel we've learned what there is to learn," said Carrie. "I've bagged a piece of the blood-stained wood from the porch. We need to take the laptop computer and zip drives. They may contain clues about who the shooter might be. We can leave the box of files you found in the closet. They contain only stuff related to the work the person living here was doing. I'll take the smart phone I found on the floor. I also have the shell casing which the Yellowstone people gave us. The shooter must be an amateur since a pro would make sure not to leave a casing. I suspect the smart phone isn't the victim's. We'll have the phone company determine who the owner is. I think the most important item is the shell casing. A first glance, it looks to be a thirty-nine caliber bullet. That means the gun is probably a kind with thousands like it in existence. We'll have the forensic folk do their thing with the casing and see what they find out. For now, I think we are done here. We can turn the place with the stuff over to Terpstra and his crew."

"Will do," responded Alex. "I'm guessing the blood will be from the woman who was shot. I did do a quick look through the files. They're about the work someone, I assume the person living here, was conducting on the Crow reservation. All kinds of references to old Crow tribal documents. There looks to be a recent entry about a sketch on an old piece of bark. Whoever prepared these files, she or he must have an interest in happenings back during the days when the Crows lived in these parts. Why the person was living here at Grant Village and doing work on the Crow reservation in Montana baffles me. Once the troops get into the laptop and zip drives, I'm sure more answers will be forthcoming. What any of it might have to do with the shooting escapes me right now. Speaking of answers, let's text Janet and find out if this is a homicide crime scene or perhaps a robbery turned violent. If it's a robbery, I agree we can turn this place over to Yellowstone Security. We will need to get permission from Janet to turn it over. We can then vamoose as soon as someone from Yellowstone Security can get here to take control of the scene. If the woman dies, however, we probably should take a second look around since it will be our homicide to investigate. I really hope we don't have to do a homicide investigation given where it happened. I, for one, don't want to have to hang around here to coordinate everything."

"Good idea. I'll text Janet. Like you, I sure hope the woman doesn't die. Besides one of us having to stay around here, I don't want to add a homicide in Yellowstone to our plate. We need to get back to monitoring our white supremacist friends, especially the two fellows who made contact with ISIS in Syria." All the agents in the Billings FBI Office were using tablets and smart phones to communicate with each other so Carrie used her phone to send Janet VanKampen photos of the inside of the cabin and a text asking about the status of the woman who had been shot. Carrie also wanted to know how she and Alex should proceed now that they had finished processing the scene. Janet must have been in between conversations or in the rare place of having a few free minutes since a reply to Carrie's text was received after only a few minutes. "*Woman in intensive care. Docs believe she will make it. Since no homicide, turn scene over to Yell security, Do a brief report. E-mail to me. I'll forward to Yell Security. MAKE IT BRIEF! Don't leave scene until Yell Security shows. Then get back to monitoring those crazies in Sandpoint.*"

"Good news," said Carrie. "Janet says the woman will probably live, so no homicide. She wants a brief report. We need to wait until someone from Yellowstone Security arrives. Then we can officially turn over the scene and investigation to them. She wants us back watching our supremacist friends.

"No homicide. That's good news," replied Alex. "So we wait until Yellowstone Security shows. Hopefully, it won't be too long a wait. You want me to do the report for Janet or do you want to do it? Makes no difference to me."

"How about you do it this time? Janet emphasized she wants it brief, so make it brief. Sounds to me like she wants to have something to cover her butt in case something unforeseen happens and questions start coming from regional or D.C. The old c.y.a. in other words. While you do a report, I'll text her back. I want to make sure she's okay with us having the Yellowstone Security people taking care of the laptop, zip drives, and files. I want to cover our rear ends in case she feels differently although I'd be surprised if she feels we should take them. It would be best, I feel, to leave them with Yellowstone Security before we head to Sandpoint."

"Okay. I don't know much about Yellowstone Security's forensic capabilities but that's not our problem. They can always request the Wyoming crime labs help them. I just wish our supremacist friends hadn't picked Sandpoint, Idaho for their headquarters. It's a long way from Billings. I assume the helicopter will take us back there."

"I'm sure it will. Let me text Janet about the laptop and other stuff. I'll tell her I'm leaving it with Yellowstone Security . You do the report. Once someone from Yellowstone Security arrives, we'll be ready to depart this place. The sooner the better as far as I'm concerned."

OFFICE OF THE ASSISTANT SUPERINTENDENT, ADMINISTRATION BUILDING, HEADQUARTERS, YELLOWSTONE NATIONAL PARK, MAMMOTH, MONTANA

"It's Director Terpstra on line one."

"Thanks, Larry," said Beth. Taking a deep breath, she tried to prepare herself for what she feared was going to be bad news. Either Marlene had died, something bad had happened to Gretchen, or both. Gripping the arm of her chair with one hand, she pressed the button for line one and lifted the phone to her ear. "Yes, Bruce. What do you have for me?"

"Beth, you said you wanted me to keep you informed about the shooting. I have good news and bad news. Which do you wish to know first?"

"If you don't mind, I'll take the good first."

"The good news is Marlene is out of danger. The docs are confident she's going to make it. It's going to be a long process of rehabilitation and strengthening, but they say she should be back to full function.

We are all so relieved and thankful. So now you really don't have to feel guilty."

Beth felt like a weight had been lifted from her shoulders. With an audible sigh, she said, "That is good news, Bruce. Wonderful news. I'm so relieved. I can't tell you how much better I feel. But, I'm still feel guilty because she's going to go through difficult times over the next several months and she wouldn't if it wasn't for me. I'm going to do something for her. I don't know what yet, but I am. There's no way she isn't going to receive all the best care and support. She will continue to receive her full salary and benefits throughout her recovery and rehabilitation, won't she?"

"You know our policies," responded Bruce. "She can use all her own sick leave until it runs out and then begin to use additional sick leave from the employee pool. That volunteer program was established several years ago and I'll check how many days are in the pool."

"I know about the sick leave pool. Every year, any sick leave days I haven't used I donate to the pool. When you find out how many days are in the pool, please let me know. If she needs more, I'll go right to the Sup and obtain whatever policy exceptions are necessary to make sure she is fully supported and doesn't lose anything in terms of salary or benefits. What about any costs associated with dependents – kids or spouse?"

"She is single," replied Bruce. "Divorced several years ago. No kids. So I don't think there are any obligations she has besides her own, but I'll check on that too."

"Good, Bruce. Now, what's the bad news?" Preparing to hear something bad about Gretchen, she was both relieved and shocked by Bruce's response.

"The bad news is there is a body of a man by the Lewis Falls parking area. A visitor found the body and had the sense to call the number on the Yellowstone brochure which is given to every visitor who enters the Park. Karen Osterhouse was the nearest ranger so she was the first person with Yellowstone to arrive at the scene. She secured it and then called us. She said it appeared to her the guy had been shot. When our people arrived, they verified the victim had been shot. He hadn't been there very long as far as we could tell. We found a shell casing near the body and it appears, just eyeballing it, to be from a bullet similar to what the shooter of Marlene used. If it is similar or actually the same type of bullet, then it wouldn't be too great a stretch to assume the same gun which was used to shoot Marlene was used in this shooting. It seems logical, then, that the shooter of this guy was the same person who shot Marlene. Of course, we won't know for sure about any of this until forensics does the actual comparison analysis. I'd be shocked if it turns out differently but we'll have to wait and see. However, if I had to bet, I'd put my money on the same gun for both shootings.

"Have you identified the man who was shot? If you're right about the shooter being the same person, then this guy who was killed might have been at Gretchen's cabin when Marlene was shot."

"The driver's license of the victim has the name Harold Boersma," responded Bruce. "We did a quick Google search and a Harold Boersma is a faculty member at Great Plains University. Another reason for calling you, Beth, is I recall you saying sometime ago that Great Plains is the university where your employee's friend is enrolled as a student. Am I right about that?"

Beth felt her heart skip a beat as she listened to Bruce give her the news about the shooting of this Boersma man. A faculty member at Great Plains. She remembered Gretchen had told her Liz was working with a professor at Great Plains. "You're correct, Bruce. Gretchen, she's my niece, was living with her friend Liz in the cabin. Gretchen told me Liz was a graduate student doing her dissertation research at Great Plains. I know from being a graduate student myself that any student doing dissertation research has a professor who oversees the student's work. Do you think there is some connection between this Boersma fellow and Liz?"

"I don't know the answer to that question, at least not yet. I have a request in to the FBI to undertake a homicide investigation since this shooting and death happened within Yellowstone; at least everything we could determine from our examination leads us to the conclusion that this is a homicide. I suspect Janet VanKampen or her agents are already doing a background search of this Boersma fellow to find out more about him and why he was in Yellowstone in the first place

Beth knew Bruce would follow proper procedures and contact the FBI. She knew the FBI had jurisdiction over homicide investigations when the homicide occurred in a national park. Bruce was correct in being cautious and doing everything according to the book. Involving the FBI was the proper thing to do. It was also the smart thing to do until it was determined if the death of this Boersma man was indeed a homicide. "When do you think you'll hear from the FBI whether or not it's a homicide investigation?"

"As soon as Janet can free up one of her agents, or maybe she will do it herself, to get to the scene of the shooting and make the determination. I hope it's sooner rather than later," replied Bruce. "I can't believe it isn't a homicide, but until the FBI makes a final determination, we shouldn't assume too much. I do know there were those two FBI agents looking into the shooting of Marlene. I know they were turning the investigation over to us but maybe they haven't left yet. If they still are in the Grant Village area, Janet might have them go to the scene of this Boersma shooting. That would make sense to me."

"What makes sense to you, Bruce, might not make sense to Janet," responded Beth. "What about Gretchen and Liz? If you are correct about the same gun being used in both shootings that says to me the same person shot both Marlene and this Boersma guy. What does it mean for Gretchen and Liz? Any reason to believe they might be involved in this Boersma shooting? I mean, any reason to think they may have been at the scene of the shooting?"

"We didn't see anything which would make us think one way or the other. There's nothing in the immediate area of the body which might hold fingerprints. Since cars park in the parking area and people walk all over the area to see the Falls, there aren't footprints we could distinguish from any others. All that's in that area are small pine trees and shrubbery. Plenty of rocks too. Really nothing to investigate but the body and the shell casing. Usually there is something, but we found nothing. However, remember ours was only a cursory look around. It's certainly possible we missed something. When the FBI does its investigating, if there is some evidence left by the shooter or anyone else who might have been there, they will find it, I'm sure."

Thanks, Bruce, please keep me informed," responded Beth. "I don't mean to make light of this Boersma fellow's death, but I'm very concerned about Gretchen. I still haven't heard from her and that is very unusual."

"Beth, I understand your concern about Gretchen. Our trace on she and Elizabeth Buikema brought nothing on Gretchen. We did receive info about Elizabeth. She's located on the Crow Reservation."

"I didn't know that," replied Beth. "Did she say anything about Gretchen? Where she might be?"

"We haven't talked with her yet but we will soon. We're hoping she can tell us about the shooting of Marlene assuming, of course, she was in the cabin when the shooting happened. What I can say is we know Elizabeth isn't missing which brings me to a suggestion. I've thought about it and concluded there is something you can do to address your concern about Gretchen. Have you thought about filing a missing person's report? We could send it to law enforcement agencies throughout Wyoming, Montana, and Idaho. They might come up with something about Gretchen. I realize you have no reason to believe she left the greater Yellowstone area, but I wouldn't rule it out if I were you."

"I suppose it wouldn't hurt," replied Beth. "The more eyes in more places the better, I suppose. I still think she's somewhere in the general Yellowstone area. There is no reason why she would leave the park. I doubt Gretchen would go with Liz to the Crow Reservation. She was working for Parker Williams as a fly fishing guide. Parker said she was booked almost every day. I'll do a missing person's report and e-mail it to you. It's a good suggestion but I don't think it will result in anything useful."

"Maybe, maybe not. But as you said, it couldn't hurt. I'll keep you informed when I learn anything more about this shooting or about Marlene."

Ending the call, Beth knew what she must do. A missing person's report wasn't going to help find Gretchen. Bruce was up to his ears with two shootings in less than twenty-four hours along with all the usual security stuff which happens in Yellowstone on a daily basis. The FBI will be focused on the shooting of this Boersma man if it turns out to be a homicide. *Finding Gretchen isn't going to be a high priority for either Bruce or Janet. I can't shake the feeling she is in trouble and needs help especially since she doesn't have Liz with her. They didn't go together into the backcountry or anywhere else, as I thought. If Gretchen is going to be found, I'm going to have to find her. I can't depend on anyone else to find her. It's up to me. I'm the one who has to find her.*

OUTSIDE CABIN 17, LOWER VILLAGE, GRANT VILLAGE, YELLOWSTONE NATIONAL PARK, WYOMING

"Alex, you aren't going to believe this. You simply aren't going to believe it," said Carrie as she shook her head in a gesture of unbelief. "What must she be thinking? This is crazy!"

Hearing Carrie raise her voice and the exasperation in her tone, Alex knew she had received a text, probably from Janet, which was not to Carrie's liking. "What am I not going to believe and who's she?"

"Janet just texted me," responded Carrie, her voice dripping with disgust. "She says forget about our supremacist friends in Idaho. She's sending us along the Lewis River near Lewis Falls. There's been another shooting. This time the victim is dead. Yellowstone Security believes it to be a homicide. Can you believe this? Two shootings in Yellowstone in less than twenty-four hours and we get stuck with both! What's going on?"

"After fifteen years with the Bureau, I'm not surprised by anything anymore," replied Alex. "Janet must have her reasons. You're right, Carrie. Two shootings back to back in Yellowstone is weird. I bet they're related. You said by Lewis Falls. That's not too far from here. We could drive if we had a vehicle. Did she say anything about how we're supposed to get there?"

As Alex was talking, Carrie's phone chirped indicating a text had arrived. Looking at the screen, she said, "It's from Janet. Here's the answer to your question. She says someone from Yellowstone will be arriving in a few minutes. The person will drive us to the scene of the shooting. The driver will know the exact location by Lewis Falls. Janet says we are to treat the shooting as a homicide. She will be sending more info as an attachment to an e-mail. She plans to send it to your tablet."

As Carrie was talking, a Chevy Tahoe drove up the gravel road and stopped in front of the cabin. The driver was dressed in the standard olive green uniform of the National Park Service. Exiting the SUV, Alex could see the driver was a young Hispanic woman, probably no older than late-twenties. She was about 5' 8", with an athletic build and jet back hair tied back in a pony tail. "Hi," she said to Alex, "you must be one of the FBI agents." As she was talking, an African-American man exited the passenger side of the Tahoe. He, too, was dressed in the uniform of the National Park Service. He looked to be in his early thirties, about 6' with muscles visible under his shirt. Thinking to himself, Alex thought, *You can't say the Yellowstone administration isn't all into diversity of its workforce.*

"Yes, I'm FBI agent Alex Ritsema. My partner is FBI agent Carrie DeLange. I assume you're here because of the shooting by Lewis Falls."

"You are correct. Emmanuel and I are with Yellowstone Security. We were told to meet two FBI agents by Cabin 17. Emmanuel is going to stay here and watch to make sure no one messes with this scene. I think you know you are turning this place over to us to carry on the investigation of the shooting that occurred here. I will drive you and Agent DeLange to the scene of the shooting by Lewis Falls. Also, if you need your own wheels after you process that scene, this Tahoe is yours to use."

"Makes sense," responded Alex, "but you didn't give me your name. Plus, I have to see some identification. It's standard procedure for the FBI. I'm sure you understand.

"Sorry about that. My name is Yolanda Martinez." Taking a small wallet from the back pocket of her slacks, she opened it and showed a Yellowstone Security photo ID. to Alex. "My partner is Emmanuel

Thomas." Emmanuel had walked to stand next to Yolanda as Carrie had done with Alex. All four exchanged handshakes.

Carrie said to Emmanuel, "Mr. Thomas, we were told someone from Yellowstone Security would take over responsibility for this crime scene. We have one matter for you to attend to and then we will be on our way. We need to see identification verifying you are who you say you are. Again, we are following FBI standard protocol. Like Ms. Martinez, I assume you carry a Yellowstone Security ID. I need to take a photo of before it we leave. Please let me see your ID."

The young man withdrew a photo ID. from the front pocket of his shirt. Taking her phone, Carrie took a photo of the it while also looking at the photo. If the ID. was a fake, whoever had done it was good since the photo was a duplicate of the young man standing before them. Carrie handed the ID. back to Emmanuel. "Mr. Thomas, this crime scene is now all yours," said Carrie. Turning to Yolanda, she continued, "Okay. Let's make tracks." Carrie, Alex, and Yolanda got into the Tahoe with Yolanda as the driver. Carrie sat in the front passenger seat while Alex went into the rear seat behind Yolanda.

"This SUV has a navigation system," said Yolanda. "Since there's only one road along the Lewis River to Lewis Falls, I don't think we need to use it. If you do use this vehicle later on, the navigation system may come in handy as I suspect you may be headed to areas with which you're unfamiliar. All set?"

Alex was impressed with this young woman's poise. He wondered about her background and any specialized training she might have participated in as a Yellowstone Security employee. He knew the FBI had instructed its agents to be on the lookout for potential recruits. At first blush, she certainly seemed to be a potential recruit. He would tell Janet about her. Janet could then decide if she wanted to forward this woman's name to the recruitment arm of the Bureau. "One last detail before we leave," responded Alex. "When we finish at the homicide scene, we plan to have a helicopter pick us up. I don't think we will need to use this SUV but its good to know it's available if we need it. Having a navigation system is certainly a plus. If we do use it, we'll leave it where we meet the helicopter. Does that work?"

"I wasn't informed about a helicopter but I'm sure it will be fine," responded Yolanda. "There aren't many open areas near where we're going where a helicopter can land so we may want to pinpoint a dry meadow near the road as we drive to the homicide scene. You could park the Tahoe near that meadow along the shoulder of the road. I'll inform the rangers in that area to be aware of a Tahoe parked somewhere on the shoulder of the road along the Lewis River."

"Good suggestion," responded Carrie. "I believe that covers everything. Anything else, Alex?"

"Not that I can think of," responded Alex from the rear seat of the Tahoe. "Let's go."

GALLATIN RIVER, YELLOWSTONE NATIONAL PARK, WYOMING

It hadn't been the best day of catching fish for the couple he was guiding. When he met them for the first time at the shop, she had expressed being nervous about wading into these white-water rivers, as she labeled the rivers in and around Yellowstone. She and her husband lived in Pella, Iowa and both had recently retired. One of the activities they had decided to undertake as a couple was fly fishing. The husband had told Parker he googled places for fly fishing in the United States and the Yellowstone region had been the highest rated of all the regions in the country. Together, they had read the reviews written by various individuals who had fly fished in the Yellowstone region. They came away convinced they would initiate their fly fishing adventures in Yellowstone. Fortunately for Parker, several of the reviews had mentioned the Gold Medal Fly Fishing Shop in West Yellowstone as the place to contact for assistance in launching a fly fishing experience. He had received an e-mail from the husband inquiring about purchasing the necessary fly fishing equipment, waders, fishing vests, and other items to outfit his wife and himself. He also inquired about having a few private lessons on the techniques of fly fishing followed by some guided fly fishing trips. Their instruction now over, it was time to put what they had learned to the test. Today was the first of several scheduled guided fly fishing trips. Parker had decided to be the guide for this trip which was their first actual fly fishing experience. He had wanted to be with them when they translated what they had learned from his instruction into actual fly fishing in a river.

Given her expressed nervousness with wading, Parker had decided to have both of them fish the Gallatin River in the northwest corner of Yellowstone rather than any of the larger rivers such as the Madison, Firehole, Fall, Lamar, or Yellowstone. The Gallatin was a calmer river than the others. It did not involve much of an elevation change which meant a slower and less powerful current. Also, the bottom of the Gallatin was fairly level with few slippery rocks to cause someone wading to be surprised and possibly lose balance. He had told the wife and husband, before they left the shop and drove to the Gallatin, that the number of fish in the river was considerably less than in the larger rivers. The fish were also smaller in size. He had wanted to prepare them for the kind of day they were most likely to experience in terms of the number and size of fish they would hopefully be catching.

The policy of the Gold Medal Fly Fishing Shop was all fish caught, regardless of size, were to be released back into the water in which they had been caught. Known as catch and release fishing, its purpose was to maintain the population of fish, which a river could sustain, and thereby ensure fish would be available for future generations of fly fishers. Fish needed to reach a certain level of maturity to be able to spawn and if too many fish were removed, especially those either able to spawn or soon to reach maturity and be able to spawn, the population would decline precipitously. Without practicing catch and release fishing, future generations of fly fishers would all too soon be fishing for fewer and fewer fish. A fish caught and not released was a fish never to reproduce again.

One reason the greater Yellowstone region was the premiere fly fishing region within the United States was that a catch and release policy existed throughout Yellowstone National Park with only a few exceptions in very limited waters. There were no exceptions to the policy when it came to Yellowstone cutthroat trout. All Yellowstone cutthroat trout were to be released back into the water immediately no matter their size or where they were caught. Significant monetary fines were leveled by Yellowstone officials on anyone having possession of a Yellowstone cutthroat trout regardless of size. Several rivers and streams had a similar policy regarding the release of rainbow and brown trout, as well as Grayling fish. Brook and lake trout, as well as whitefish, were exceptions to the catch and release policy. In most rivers and streams, a couple of brook trout could be kept. The one species of trout for which an opposite policy was operational, call it a policy of catch and kill, was lake trout. All lake trout were to be killed. None were to be allowed to live. This was due to the fact that lake trout were vicious predators of all other species of fish. Lake trout was an invasive species in Yellowstone. No one had yet been able to determine how lake trout had been introduced into Yellowstone Lake. But, as a predator, lake trout wrecked havoc on the native populations of cutthroat trout, reducing their population by nearly ninety percent. Cutthroat trout used Yellowstone Lake as a "holding pen" before moving into rivers and streams to spawn. They were not aggressive nor were they predatorial which made them easy pickings for the aggressive, predatory lake trout. A million dollars a year was being spent by the Yellowstone administration to eradicate lake trout from Yellowstone Lake in the hope of restoring cutthroat trout to levels where various species of animals – bears, otters, eagles, and osprey – which depended on their availability as a primary food source, would once again find sufficient numbers moving out of Yellowstone Lake into many feeder streams throughout the year. Lake trout did not move out of Yellowstone Lake but stayed deep in the water where animals were unable to reach them. Hence, with no natural predator, lake trout multiplied exponentially and killed thousands of cutthroat trout every year.

For two inexperienced fly fishers, the number of fish caught and released was satisfactory, Parker thought. The wife expressed herself several times regarding how much she was enjoying her fishing experience. That's all Parker needed to hear. If she was happy, her husband would be happy. She hadn't slipped while wading and her confidence had increased once Parker showed her how to use her wading staff as a means to provide extra stability walking in the water. Both she and her husband were good students. They listened to the tips and suggestions Parker gave about where and how to find fish in certain areas of the river. The result was that they each caught several fish. They showed their gratitude by adding a substantial gratuity to the normal fee the Gold Medal Fly Fishing Shop charged for a personal guided wading trip for two people. They also talked Parker into guiding them the next day on another wading trip to Soda Butte Creek. Soda Butte Creek held a substantial population of Yellowstone cutthroat trout and Parker knew catching and releasing some would be a bonus for the couple.

OFFICE OF THE ASSISTANT SUPERINTENDENT, ADMINISTRATION BUILDING, HEADQUARTERS, YELLOWSTONE NATIONAL PARK, MAMMOTH, MONTANA

Don't panic. Take deep breaths. Losing it won't do any good. I can't let myself go all to pieces. I need to keep it together. Yesterday afternoon's news about the body of the man by Lewis Falls had pushed her past the normal levels of concern and anxiety for the whereabouts and security of Gretchen. With very little hope, she felt something terribly wrong had happened and Gretchen was caught in it. What little positive there was in such a horrible situation was now that the FBI was investigating the shooting, at least until the cause of the poor guy's death was officially determined, the resources the FBI could bring to bare would dramatically increase the probability of locating Gretchen, assuming she was being held by whomever had probably killed the man. If Gretchen had been kidnapped by a murderer, why she had been kidnapped perplexed Beth. Now that an apparent murder had occurred, coupled with Gretchen's disappearance, Beth was pushed to near panic. Worry, anxiety, frustration, fear, and feelings of helplessness all contributed to her despair. *I can't just sit here and do nothing. I can't rely on the FBI or our security folk to find Gretchen. Waiting for a phone call or text message telling me no progress has been made will just cause me more anxiety and drive me into depression. I have to get going myself.* Picking up the office phone, she pushed the button for the Superintendent's administrative assistant. Her call was answered after two rings. "Superintendent's office, Brenda speaking. How may I direct your call?"

"Hi, Brenda, it's Beth. Please do me a favor. Please tell the Sup I'm taking a personal leave of absence, starting immediately. Also, I don't know how long my absence might be. I'll stay in touch as best I can."

"Assistant Superintendent Richardson, is something wrong? Are you okay? You sound upset and very anxious."

"I'm okay, but I have to attend to something that's come up and it can't wait. I'm sorry if this creates a problem for our leader, but I have no other option but to immediately take leave. I'll have Larry cancel or reschedule my appointments and meetings. Please tell our leader not to worry about me. As I said, I'm okay. I'll be in touch." Ending the call before any more questions could be asked, she closed her eyes and tried to concentrate on how she should proceed. *I need to find out more about the man who was killed and anyone else that might be involved with Gretchen's disappearance, assuming she didn't take off on her own. Knowing something about folks involved in this calamity might provide a clue why Gretchen went missing in the first place and where she may be now.* Picking up her phone again, she pushed the button for the Security Office. After a few rings, a female answered whose voice Beth recognized.

"Yellowstone Security Office. Maria speaking. How may I help you?"

"Hi, Maria. It's Beth Richardson. Is Bruce available?"

"Hello, Assistant Superintendent Richardson. I'm sorry, Director Terpstra isn't here. He's meeting with a couple of FBI agents at a crime scene by Lewis Falls. Are you aware what happened there?"

"Yes, I have some knowledge but I'd prefer to hear more about it directly from Bruce. I assume he can be reached via his mobile phone?"

"Yes. Do you have his number?"

"I do. Thanks Maria. I'll give him a call." Taking her own phone from the zippered inside pocket of her uniform blouse, she found

Bruce's phone number on her contacts list. She pushed the call button. After several rings, she recognized Bruce's voice.

"Hello."

"Bruce, it's Beth."

"Hey, Beth. What's up?"

"Maria said you're with some FBI agents at the place of the shooting. I know the FBI is involved and I also know getting any information from them is like pulling teeth. If this isn't a good time for you to talk with me for a few minutes, you can call me back as soon as you're free. What I need to know is what you can tell me about the who, what, when, and why of the shooting and the happenings surrounding it."

"You're right about the FBI. Don't quote me, but the agents here don't seem to be too interested in the situation. They aren't too happy that they were diverted from another case they are working. I overheard them grumbling about it. I've the feeling they would rather not have me here at all. They aren't paying any attention to me so we can talk now."

"Great. I totally understand how the FBI ignores everyone but their own. Real elitists in terms of law enforcement. No one else measures up to them is how they think and act. Sometimes I think it would be better if the FBI delegated more and wasn't so tight-lipped. I could go on and on about the FBI, as I'm sure you could do as well, but let's leave that for another day. Please tell me what you know."

"You already know the victim was Harold Boersma. He was a professor at Great Plains University. We knew that before the FBI took over. Since these two FBI agents showed up, no additional information about this Boersma fellow has been forthcoming. If they have information, they aren't sharing it. If this Boersma fellow was involved with Elizabeth Buikema, and I don't mean anything other than in a professor/graduate student way, the FBI agents haven't said. I suspect she and Boersma at least knew each other. They may have had a mutual research interest. Otherwise, why would he be in an area close to where she lived? But, it's speculation on my part. Sorry I can't give you any more specific information, especially about Gretchen."

"I'm not surprised the FBI isn't sharing information. Once they take over an investigation, they see no reason to keep the underlings informed. Their superior attitude drives me crazy, but it's what it is. Any guesses about any of the other people who might have been there when the shooting happened? I'm particularly interested if you think Gretchen might have been there."

"I've no idea. Your guess is as good as mine. Sorry. As I said, I don't have any information about who might have been with this Boersma fellow. If these FBI agents know something about that, they're not saying. As I said, they don't seem to be very concerned. But, I'll try to find out more and let you know if I learn anything significant."

"Thanks, Bruce, and please do keep me informed. Don't hesitate to call me." Hearing about the so-so attitude of the FBI agents only added to her realization she had to pursue finding Gretchen herself. She couldn't rely on the FBI or even Bruce to find Gretchen because, it dawned on her, there was no real evidence proving Gretchen was being held against her will or had even been at the scene of the shooting. Gretchen was, at best, a missing person and not necessarily missing against her own will. *I could be making a mountain out of a molehill. But, I need to find Gretchen regardless. Not knowing if she is okay is driving me crazy.*

SODA BUTTE CREEK, NORTHEAST YELLOWSTONE NATIONAL PARK, WYOMING

The husband and wife who had hired him to guide them fishing Soda Butte Creek had been explicit about their desire to fish for Yellowstone cutthroat trout. Parker knew, from experience, Soda Butte Creek was home to a sizable population of Yellowstone cutthroat trout. Soda Butte Creek was the ideal stream for them to fish since they were completely okay with not catching huge fish or a large number of fish. Catching a few fish of average size was perfectly acceptable with them. Soda Butte Creek provided beautiful surroundings while fishing for fish in the eleven to fifteen inch range, large enough to provide a satisfying fight before being released to be caught another time in the future.

As he watched his clients fish, he thought again how more women were now fly fishers. Since opening the Gold Medal Fly Fishing Shop and providing fly fishing instruction and guide services to clients, ranging from beginners to experienced individuals, he had witnessed an increasing number of women engaged in the sport. The percentages of female and male fly fishers was becoming closer to fifty-fifty. Consequently, employing women guides had become an increasingly important priority for all fly fishing businesses offering guide services. He felt very fortunate and was grateful to Beth for suggesting Gretchen to him as a candidate to become a guide for his business. She had worked out well. She had caught on quickly to the requirements of guiding and had been reliable until now. *She has to be reliable if she expects me to continue to employ her. I can't have her not showing up after booking women clients who explicitly request a female guide.* He wondered if Beth had learned anything about where Gretchen had gone. *Maybe I should call Beth to find out what she has learned.* Reaching for his phone, he was interrupted by a shout.

"This one's good size," said Marcie, the woman client. "It took that March Brown soft hackle at the bottom of the swing drift, just as you said. Look at that jump!" Watching her, Parker could see she had learned not to be too forceful with the fish but also not play it too long to exhaustion. Playing a fish too long would result in the fish dying because of over exhaustion and not being able to recover. Knowing how to play the fish, when to bring it to net, and how to carefully handle and release it was acquired through experience. Parker made it a habit to provide instruction on the proper handling of fish to all clients of the shop. He showed them the proper way to play the fish from when it was first hooked to being released. However, talking about it and actually doing it were two different matters. It usually required several experiences to get it down. As Parker watched Marcie bring the fish closer to her and get ready to slide her net under it, he could see the bright red slash of color along the gills of the fish. Sure enough, it was a Yellowstone cutthroat trout. Continuing to watch, he was pleased how carefully Marcie handled the fish and gently worked it back and forth sideways in the water to stimulate the gills and increase its utilization of oxygen in the water passing through its gills. Standing by her, he checked the soft hackle March Brown fly she was using. It had held up well during the gyrations of the trout as it tried to decrease the pressure on it from the tautness of the fishing line and leader connected to the fly. Parker knew it was a common misunderstanding that fish felt pain from the hook. Not so. What the fish felt and fought to rid itself of was the pressure limiting its freedom of movement. Being able to move at will with total freedom of movement to being very limited with pressure against its head resulted in the fight by the fish which everyone who fished sought as the epitome of the fishing experience.

"You're good to go again," said Parker to Marcie. "Cast the fly in the same way you did before. Allow it to drift, swinging across and down from you, and be ready for a fish to strike at the bottom of the swing when the fly is straight down current from you. Remember, count three seconds – one one thousand, two one thousand, three one thousand – before lifting the fly from the water and doing it all over again. Trout often strike at the very bottom of the drift."

"I didn't know fly fishing could be this much fun," replied Marcie. "I also didn't realize it's part science and part art. Call it skill, I guess." Pointing toward her husband, whose fly rod was bent and shaking, "Look," she exclaimed, "Allen has one on. I think it's his fifth or sixth." Allen had shown Parker he knew how to land and release a fish, so Parker let him be. Both Marcie and Allen had translated the instruction Parker had given them into successful fishing. He felt he could let them be on their own while he called Beth. Taking his phone from the inside pocket of his fishing vest, he found both Beth's office and mobile phone numbers. He tried her office number first. His call was answered by Larry Hoogstrate, Beth's administrative assistant.

"Assistant Superintendent Richardson's office, Larry speaking." The formality of the Yellowstone administrative offices and personnel continued to amaze Parker. "Why so formal?" he had once asked Beth. She had replied with a shrug of her shoulders and said tradition dictated certain matters within the Yellowstone administration. Referencing officials of the administration with their titles was one such tradition. According to Beth, the Superintendent hadn't wanted to fight the battle of trying to establish a more relaxed atmosphere so the formality continued.

"Good afternoon, Larry. it's Parker Williams. Might Beth be available for a few minutes?"

"I'm afraid she's on leave, Doctor Williams. When she calls in, which I'm sure she will, I can let her know you called."

He cringed whenever someone used "doctor" when addressing him. Sure, he had a Ph.D. in biology, but what difference did it make now that he was away from university and academic life? He knew a whole lot about plants, insects, and biological processes, but it contributed little to operating a successful retail and service business. Some university and college faculty, with egos as big as barns and inflated opinions of themselves, cared if people knew they had a Ph.D. degree. "Okay Larry, when you hear from her, please tell her I called and would like her to call back. In the meantime, I'll try her mobile." He found Beth's mobile phone number and pressed the call button. After several rings, her voice message answered. *This is Beth. Please leave your message and I'll call you back. Enjoy your day.* "Beth, it's Parker. I'm concerned about you since I heard from Larry you are on leave. Why on leave? Are you okay? Is there something wrong? Please call me when you can. I'd like to help if I can. I need to hear from you." He realized she wasn't obligated to tell him before making a decision; they weren't at that level in their relationship. But they usually shared plans with each other about vacations or travel. Neither of them had family nearby so they relied on each other to know about the other person's whereabouts. Not day-to-day stuff, but certainly absences of a few days. She hadn't said anything to him about plans to be away. *Not like her. Something's not right. I wonder if she heard from Gretchen and took off to meet her.* His thoughts were interrupted by a question from Allen.

"Parker, can you help me? I need a replacement fly. My March Brown was kind of chewed apart by that last cutthroat. Shall I try a different fly or stick with a March Brown?"

Wading over to Allen, Parker replied, "No reason to switch to a different fly. I always say stick to what's working. You've been doing well with a March Brown so let me tie on another for you." Smiling and with a joking voice, he continued, "Marcie's a few fish ahead of you and you don't want her bragging about how she out-fished you, so I wouldn't change flies now. Stick with what's working until it doesn't anymore." Taking a size 14 March Brown soft hackle from his fly box, Parker tied it to the end of the 4x tippet which, in turn, was tied to the end of the 2x leader connected to Allen's fly line. The fly line, which Parker had recommended Allen purchase, was a Rio Gold, all-purpose, floating fly line. It was loaded onto a Sage fly reel which, in turn, was attached to a Sage fly rod, both Parker's number one recommended fly fishing rod and reel. He had fished with numerous fly rods and reels from various manufacturers throughout the years. After evaluating them all, he felt the Sage rods and reels were number one. Similarly, he rated waders, wading boots, and fishing clothes manufactured by Simms, a fly fishing manufacturer in Bozeman, Montana, as number one in those categories. Turning back toward where Marcie was bringing another fish to her net, he heard his phone buzz. He hoped it was Beth returning his call. Taking the phone from the inside zippered pocket of his vest, he said, "This is Parker."

"Hi, Parker, it's Beth. I got your message. Thanks for caring. I'm okay, at least physically, but I'm not so sure about emotionally or mentally. I'm worried sick about Gretchen, especially now with the murder yesterday. I haven't heard..."

"What did you say? Murder? What murder? Who was murdered? What does it...?

"That's just it," replied Beth. "I hardly know anything about it. All I know from talking with Bruce is a man's body was found by Lewis Falls. He'd been shot dead. His name is Boersma and he is a professor at Great Plains University. Bruce thinks, and I tend to agree with him, this Boersma fellow and Liz probably knew each other because of Liz' research. Bruce is also thinking the murder of this guy and the shooting of Marlene are connected, maybe even the same shooter. Forensics needs to provide a precise answer but Bruce thinks the same type bullets were used for both shootings. His preliminary conclusion is the same gun was probably used which means the same shooter probably shot both Marlene and this Boersma fellow. I'm really worried there is a connection between his murder and Gretchen's disappearance. I'm only speculating about a connection but I can't shake the thought that Gretchen is somehow in the middle of this and may be in trouble. I've decided I have to take it upon myself to try and find her. Maybe there's no connection. Maybe I'm creating a federal case out of nothing. What I do know is I couldn't live with myself if I did nothing and later found out I could have helped find Gretchen or get her out of trouble."

Parker didn't like where she was headed. Responding, he asked, "So, where are you now and what are you planning to do?"

"Right now, I'm packing the Tahoe with enough stuff to last me several days in the backcountry. Call it woman's intuition, but my gut tells me Gretchen is somewhere in the Yellowstone backcountry in the general vicinity of the southeast region of the park. My gut tells me she is being held by the shooter of Marlene and the killer of this Boersma guy. I know, I know, before you say it, I realize I've no evidence to support my belief. I believe it anyway and I'm going to act on my belief. Where she might be in this area of Yellowstone is a good guess. I have no idea. I'm going to try and find some clue as to where she might have been taken in that area."

He really didn't like what she was saying. He needed to change her mind. "Beth, you can't go alone into the backcountry. You know that's against everything you believe and preach. Backcountry travel, especially camping, needs to be done by at least two people together. You know the risks and dangers of being alone in the Yellowstone backcountry. You simply can't go alone, especially if you're correct and she's being held by a murderer. You just can't go alone. You really don't know where to go. If Gretchen is being held in the backcountry, who knows where that might be. She could be anywhere. Let the authorities do the searching."

"I know what you are saying about going into the backcountry and you're right. I know we preach safety above everything which means no going into the backcountry alone overnight. I wouldn't be doing this if I didn't think it was absolutely necessary. Do you think Janet is going to have her agents look for Gretchen? Sure, if there was evidence Gretchen was being held by the person who shot Marlene and killed this Boersma guy, Janet would be searching for Gretchen while searching for the shooter. Unfortunately, there isn't any evidence. Janet certainly isn't going to follow a hunch by me. She needs evidence. Then there's Bruce. He doesn't have the resources to devote to helicopter fly-overs or horseback search parties. Even if he could devote some resources, as I just said, there's no real evidence to show Gretchen has been kidnapped or was around the shooting of Boersma or is even being held against her will. Sorry, Parker, thanks for your concern. You know how much I value your opinion and especially your support. You know my feelings for you and, believe me, I don't want anything to jeopardize our relationship. I'll certainly be careful, but I'm going. I can't just sit around and hope Gretchen will show up. As soon as I finish getting my stuff organized and into the Tahoe, I'm going to go to Grant Village. I'm going to go through Liz and Gretchen's cabin with a fine tooth comb. I know the FBI checked it for clues but I need to see for myself if there may be some clue where Gretchen may have gone, either willingly or under duress. The FBI people might have overlooked something or didn't realize what they're looking at was a clue."

She's not being rational about this. She thinks she's going to find something important when the FBI didn't. "What do you expect to find? I'm sure the FBI went through the cabin carefully. If there was anything important, those agents would've found it. They're trained and have experience in searching for clues."

"You may be right about the expertise of the FBI agents. Then again, maybe they weren't as focused as I'm intending to be. They would've concentrated on looking for clues related to the shooting of Marlene, not on Gretchen's disappearance. Besides, whatever Janet or her agents do or don't do is beyond my control. What I can control is what I do. So the first thing I can do is check out Liz and Gretchen's cabin. Even though I don't want to do it, I'm going to contact those two FBI agents who searched the cabin. Bruce has their names. I want to know what they learned from their search."

Knowing how useless it would be to continue to argue with her – he had been there before with Beth and had experienced her unwillingness to listen to reason – he decided to try another approach. "Beth, how about I join you? I'll feel much better about you being in the backcountry if you're not alone. I'd be worried sick knowing you were alone. Besides, I wasn't so bad to be with the last time we were together in the Yellowstone backcountry, was I?"

Laughing, she responded, "No, you weren't so bad. In a mocking tone of voice, she continued, "Perhaps you've conveniently forgotten how you forgot to stake your tent securely so we had to chase it across that meadow at three in the morning? And are you also conveniently forgetting how you had to borrow a pair of my socks since you forgot yours? Kidding aside, you know my answer. Of course, I'd love to have you join me. It's very thoughtful and considerate of you. But, if you think you're going to change my mind by stalling around or trying to point out all the negatives, then please don't join me. As I said, I'll be careful. I'm certainly willing to go by myself."

In a sarcastic tone of voice he responded, "I wouldn't think of trying to change your mind. I haven't been successful before when I tried, so why would I be now? Seriously, I really don't want you to be alone in the Yellowstone backcountry. Maybe you're right about Gretchen. Hopefully, we can find her and help her if she needs help. Tell you what. I'll be finished with my two clients shortly. They have their own car so I can go directly from here to my place to get my stuff. I'll meet you as soon as I can at Grant Village."

"Sounds great. Your consideration means a lot to me. I assume you remember the cabin number is 17. I'll wait for you there. Oh yes, one more thing. Please don't forget socks this time."

OFFICE OF HAROLD BOERSMA, GREAT PLAINS UNIVERSITY, MADISON POINT, MONTANA

"I guess that does it," said Carrie. "Nothing much here to link this guy to any suspicious stuff. He certainly wasn't a happy camper about being shut out of grant money by the administration. In terms of why he was murdered, I didn't find anything. How about you?"

"Same here. I didn't find anything in this place to raise questions. The answers to why he was in the Lewis Falls area and got himself killed aren't here," replied Alex. "However, there is something which caught my eye, but not about the murder scene. It's about that cabin back at Grant Village. Bruce Terpstra said a woman graduate student was living there with another woman. She was doing historical research related to mineral rights associated with Native American tribes living in the Yellowstone region. Remember all those files in the cabin? That's what they involved. I didn't think anything of it at the time but I remember seeing the Great Plains University logo on several of the documents in those files. The woman living in the cabin and this Boersma guy were both involved in the same area of study and research at the same university. Coincidental? Maybe, maybe not. I don't hold much stock in coincidences, so maybe there's something here. Take a look at this one file I found on his desk under a stack of papers." Handing the file to Carrie, he continued, "Tell me if you smell some potential relationship between our Professor Boersma and the woman who is named Elizabeth Buikema. Unless, I'm reading too much into this, he was her research professor. Maybe he was more than that as well."

Skimming the papers in the file, Carrie responded, "I think you might be on to something. For sure this Boersma fellow and this Elizabeth Buikema were professor and student. Was there more than a professor-student relationship? As you said, maybe, maybe not. It might have been purely academic. I think we need to verify this relationship before we go much further. We need to know for sure the names of the women living in the cabin and if one of them is this Elizabeth Buikema. I'll call Bruce Terpstra. In the meantime, you text Janet and tell her what we are checking and why."

Each took their mobile phone. Carrie engaged in a brief conversation with Bruce Terpstra, shaking her head up and down during the conversation. Seeing Carrie shaking her head, indicating she received a positive response from Bruce to her inquiry, Alex sent a text to Janet briefly telling her about their discovery. "Next stop is Boersma's apartment. The listing in the university's website for addresses of its faculty is 2578 Florence Street. We'll let the GPS guide us there. Before we go, let's make sure this office stays off limits to everyone. Let's yellow tape the door and tell the university security office to make sure everyone stays out of here until we say it is okay to enter it."

"I was hoping we wouldn't have to run this investigation," said Carrie. "Not that I have anything against Yellowstone, but commuting to and from Billings doesn't make much sense. Having to stay in one of those cabins at Grant Village doesn't excite me either. I'd have to make arrangements for my kid and that is a huge pain to say nothing of the expense. If you feel the same way as I do, I'm going to request...maybe plead or beg is a better way to describe how I'm going to approach Janet...to assign someone else to do the investigating."

"I'd like nothing better than to turn this over to someone else," responded Alex. "I have my own set of problems with both the commute from Billings and staying overnight some place, Those short beds at Grant Village don't cut it. Janet knows how much we have on our plate already. Besides, Yellowstone Security personnel could accomplish much of the grunt work which we would have to do. Use all those persuasive powers you possess and get us out of this investigation. I'm counting on you, partner."

OFFICE OF THE FBI, BILLINGS, MONTANA

Killing two birds with one stone. What could be better? Carrie and Alex will owe me and I can use it to my advantage later on. Plus, I'll have a legitimate reason for being in contact with Parker and having him spend time with me on this case. I'll deputize him again like I did before. I'll make it so he and I meet to review the progress of the investigation and decide next steps. What I don't know is whether Parker will have time to work on this case. If he does, will he agree to do so? I better call him and see what he says. She knew he would want to know what Carrie and Alex told her about what they had learned. He would also ask what her expectations were for his involvement. *I have to be careful. I can't make it obvious that being with him is my primary motivation for deputizing him and having him involved in this case. Being together will occur naturally as the case unfolds. I don't have to push it now.* She kept personal telephone numbers on her phone so she went to her contact list, found Parker's personal number, and pushed "call". After several rings, his answering message responded. "Hello. Please leave your message." "Typical Parker," she thought. "Short; to the point; no other information."

"Hi, Parker. This is Janet. Long time no talk. I have an opportunity for you. Please call me as soon as you can, either my office or personal number. Look forward to hearing from you."

As he drove into Grant Village, his phone rang. *I should answer it but I'll wait until I get to the cabin in case it's Beth calling. Maybe she got hung up and won't be here for awhile. On the other hand, it might be Lori or Dick calling. Something may have come up at the shop and they need to check with me.* As he neared Cabin 17, he saw Beth's Honda CR-V parked by it. *Beth isn't here yet. Maybe it was her calling. I'd better check.* Taking his phone and accessing the message, he was surprised when he didn't hear Beth's voice, but Janet's. He listened to the message which made him both curious and concerned. *Opportunity. What opportunity? Janet most likely had numerous investigations going on. If she means my getting involved in something like that, I can't. I'm going with Beth. That's what I'm committed to do. I better call Janet back so she knows I'm not available.* His phone rang again before he had found the number for the FBI's Billings office. Looking at the phone screen, he saw it was Beth calling. "Hi Beth. What's up?"

"I'm just passing Cascade Falls. I'm going to be a little late in getting there. Traffic problems around Biscuit Basin and Old Faithful. I didn't want you to worry."

"No problem. I just arrived here myself. No vehicles are here except for your Honda. I guess Bruce must have hauled the Subaru that was here to the holding pen. Did he find out the owner of it? Anyway, I'll wait until you get here before going into the cabin. I assume you have a passkey so we can get in."

"I've the grand master for Grant Village on my key ring. I should be there in about thirty minutes or so unless I run into a herd of bison enjoying a leisurely walk down the highway. Now that you mention it, I should ask Bruce what he learned about the owner of the Subaru. I'll do that when I talk with him. See you soon."

I've some time before Beth arrives. I have to admit being involved in some of the FBI's investigations and even being deputized as a temporary FBI agent has been intriguing and enjoyable. A nice diversion from my usual daily activities. Janet has made all of it possible. He found the number for the Billings FBI office and called it.

"Federal Bureau of Investigation. How may I direct your call?"

He recognized the voice of Alice VanderArk, Janet's administrative assistant. Alice had moved from Muskegon, Michigan several years earlier where she had been the administrative assistant to the Special Agent in Charge of the mid-Michigan FBI office. "Hi Alice. It's Parker. Janet called and asked me to call back."

"Parker, it's good to hear from you. I trust all is well with you. I recommended you to a couple from Alabama who live here in the summer. They wanted to have some instruction in fly fishing before they tried their hand fly fishing in Yellowstone."

"Thanks for the recommendation, Alice. If they already called the shop, I personally didn't talk with them. Lori or Dick probably did. Next time I talk with either, I'll ask them if they have talked with your couple. Do you remember their names?"

"Yes. Peter and Margie DeYoung. They bought a house down the street from us. I met them at a neighborhood get together. Of course, all of us having lived in Michigan made conversation easy."

"I'll let you know if Lori or Dick heard from them. Now, is Janet available?"

"I'll put her on. Hold for a second."

He waited for several seconds before Janet came on the line. "Hi, Parker. Thanks for returning my call. It certainly has been awhile. How is life?"

"You mean business or personal? One's good; the other I'm not so sure about."

"That doesn't sound good. What's the trouble?"

"I know you're already involved with the two shootings in Yellowstone, the last one looking very much like a homicide. If the word gets out suggesting Yellowstone isn't a safe place to visit, my business, as well as all the businesses reliant on visitors to Yellowstone, will suffer. That isn't why I answered your question as I did. One of my employees, a young woman who guides for me, is somehow tied up, I think, in the shootings. How, I've no idea. What concerns me is she is missing. She hasn't responded to numerous calls and texts. The first shooting, the one involving the Yellowstone employee, occurred at the cabin where my employee and her friend live. So, you can understand why I'm worried and concerned."

"That's interesting and also very coincidental. Call it ESP, Parker. I called you because of the second shooting, the homicide one, which you know means it's in my lap. I have to do the investigation. I can ask Bruce to do some of it but ultimately it is my responsibility. Consequently, I need eyes and ears on it."

"Do you think the two shootings are connected? I assume you already have some agents investigating the homicide shooting."

"It's too early to know if the two shootings are related. We're no longer involved with the first shooting since it isn't a homicide. As for the homicide, I assigned Carrie Delange and Alex Ritsema. Two of my best agents. I believe you know both. However, they can't continue. They're in the middle of a very big and potentially explosive public relations nightmare involving some possible domestic terrorists with ISIS leanings. So, I'm in a bind. That's why I called you. I need your help. Big time. I want to deputize you. Have you continue where Carrie and Alex leave off. I'll be able to personally provide you with some assistance but you will be the lead. I wouldn't ask you if I wasn't in such a pinch. These ridiculous visits by presidential candidates, coupled with all the cases on our plate right now, have overwhelmed us. I really need your help. I wouldn't ask you if I didn't really need you. Can you do it?"

Janet had caught him off guard. His first inclination was not to do it because of the responsibility that went along with being the head honcho of a FBI investigation. Plus, he had made a commitment to Beth to go with her. He couldn't reneg on Beth, not this late. On the other hand, being able to call upon the resources of the FBI, as Beth and he were searching for Gretchen, could potentially be an enormous help. He could justify searching for Gretchen as part of the FBI investigation of the homicide since Gretchen may have been present during the shooting of the Boersma fellow. She would then be a valuable witness and might be the key to solving the homicide. She needed to be located so she could tell what happened, assuming she had been present at the shooting. Beth and he could use whatever assistance he could wrangle out of the FBI, although he couldn't think what that might be at this stage of the game. "Before I say I'll do it, let me describe what I have in mind. You then tell me if it's okay with you and if you still want me to proceed. I believe an employee of mine, Gretchen VanderSluis is her name, is mixed up in both shootings. She could hold the key to apprehending the shooter and solving both shootings. Finding Gretchen is paramount, I feel. I'm going to concentrate on finding Gretchen. If I'm right and she has information about the homicide shooting, that would be the best of both worlds."

"Makes sense to me," responded Janet. "Let me know if and when you need something from me. Otherwise, I'm going to concentrate on these presidential candidate visits and the other investigations we have. Do you still have your temporary FBI credentials from the last time you were deputized?"

"I still have everything. One more thing. Now that I'm ready to be involved there's one more matter you should know about. Gretchen is my employee and she is also the daughter of a cousin of Beth Richardson. Beth is already searching for Gretchen. She will probably join me at some time since we both will be looking for the same person."

"Well, both of you searching for the same person means more eyes, so that's a plus. I want to emphasize that solving the homicide is why I'm deputizing you. Your focus must be on that, not necessarily finding your employee, although I agree she may well be a key to solving the homicide. As this moves along, you and I will need to meet now and then, so keep in touch."

"Okay, Janet, I understand. Solving the homicide is the objective. Shall I send text messages to you to keep you informed?"

"That will work. We also will need to meet occasionally. When my schedule allows, I'll be able to come to Yellowstone. One of our choppers can get me there quite quickly. Bruce also has a couple choppers which you or I can use. We'll be able to get together when we need to."

"Okay. How about sending me all the information you have regarding the homicide? No sense in my reinventing the wheel. Send it to my phone."

"Will do and thanks, Parker. Good luck."

CABIN 17, LOWER VILLAGE, GRANT VILLAGE, YELLOWSTONE NATIONAL PARK, WYOMING

He saw a Yellowstone Chevy Tahoe driving down the gravel road leading to Cabin 17. *Here comes Beth. I need to tell her about Janet's call and my role in investigating the homicide.* Beth exited her Tahoe as he walked toward her. Reaching her, she pulled him to her in a hug. "Thank you for being willing to help me search for Gretchen. It means a great deal to me."

"It's what good friends do," responded Parker as they broke their hug. "There's something I want you to know before we develop our plan for finding Gretchen." He told her about Janet's call, her request of him, his being deputized, and leading the investigation.

"We can certainly use all the resources and help available," responded Beth. "Let's go into the cabin and see if we find something to help us find Gretchen." Taking a key from her blouse pocket, she opened the front door of the cabin. Entering, he could see the interior had already been searched. The information Janet had sent included the results from Carrie and Alex's search of the cabin. He doubted Beth and he would find anything more than what Carrie and Alex had included in their report but he did want to check out one item. He thought maybe Carrie and Alex might not have realized something about where Gretchen may have gone since the focus of their search was the shooting, not the disappearance of Gretchen.

"Beth, why don't you look through what's still here from Gretchen's personal stuff. You may find something which will help us but didn't mean anything to Carrie and Alex. I want to look through the work files which Carrie and Alex mentioned in their report. If I can find a work plan or something which indicates what Liz planned to do next, perhaps it involved Gretchen. Unless you have a better idea, we can begin with that."

"I don't have a better idea. Let's hope one of us finds something useful," replied Beth. "I'm sure the drawers were all searched by Carrie and Alex but I doubt the pockets of Gretchen's or Liz's clothes were searched."

They went about their searches without much communication. If either had found something important, neither told the other. Parker realized the files he was reviewing were a chronology of Liz's work in implementing her dissertation's research topic. The last few files contained Liz's description of her work in an area different from where she had concentrated until a few weeks earlier. The last few weeks she had focused her efforts on learning about the happenings in a Crow Native American village governed by a chief named Swift Eagle. Her records indicated she had found historical documents showing the famous explorer, John Colter, had lived in the village and established a friendship with Swift Eagle. The last file, which Parker assumed was chronologically the most recent, suggested Liz had discovered a sketch showing where this Crow chief had hidden pieces of rock which might contain gold nuggets. Liz had written in the margin of the paper she thought the hiding place was near a lake and the waterfall of a river in the southern section of Yellowstone. He knew of several waterfalls in that area of Yellowstone. Two in particular. The Fall River Falls and Lewis River Falls were large waterfalls with, of course, rivers feeding them. Other smaller waterfalls feed by smaller streams and creeks dotted the area too. The only one close to a lake, however, was Lewis Falls.

"I didn't find anything useful," said Beth, as she walked over to where Parker was still looking through the file. "How about you? Did you find anything useful?"

"I'm not sure. I want your opinion. Take a look through what is in this file. It might be a place for us to start searching. It's a guess. I have nothing but a gut feeling about this." Handing the file to her, he continued, "Here, you look through this file. Tell me your opinion."

SECURITY OFFICE, ADMINISTRATION BUILDING, HEADQUARTERS YELLOWSTONE NATIONAL PARK, MAMMOTH, MONTANA

"Director Terpstra. Assistant Director Hoogstrate is on line two. I think she is calling with an update on Marlene."

"Thanks, Shirley." Pressing the line two button on the phone, he said, "Alice, I hope you have good news."

"I do, Bruce, I do. Marlene is out of the woods. She is going to make it for sure. She's being moved from intensive care as we speak. The doctors won't say how long she needs to stay here but it's going to be several more days. She should be cognizant enough in a few hours to be interviewed. Unless you tell me differently, I plan to stay here and interview her when she's settled in her room. I'm hoping she can tell us something useful about the shooting."

"That's wonderful news. I'm so relieved. For sure, Alice, stay there. If you can talk with her, all the better. Hopefully, she will remember the shooting. As you know, the mind often blocks out trauma. She might not remember anything about the shooting. You may need to try to jog her memory. You may have to coax her along. Even if she can't remember, the best thing is she's on the mend. What are the doctors saying about her recovery? Will she have a full recovery?"

"Bruce, you know how doctors are. Closed mouth and non-committal. All I can get them to say is that she's stable and now needs to rebuild her strength. After that she'll need to be weaned off the pain medication. That's all they say. Typical doctors. They think no information is better than providing some information. Of course, the lawyers don't help. They pounce on anything a doctor might say which really shuts them down from saying much."

"Okay, Alice. Thanks for hanging in there. You're right about the doctors, lawyers too. Keep me updated." Knowing Beth Richardson was, most likely, still harboring guilt about sending Marlene to that cabin in the first place, he buzzed Shirley.

"Yes."

"Please try to reach Beth. Your intuition was right on. Marlene is stable and out of intensive care."

"That's wonderful news," responded Shirley. "I'll call Assistant Superintendent Richardson's office right now." It was less than one minute and he was buzzed. "Assistant Superintendent Richardson is on leave. I said if she called in to tell her you wanted to talk with her."

Taking his mobile phone from his shirt pocket, he found Beth's mobile phone number and called it. After several rings, her answering message started. When it finished, he left a message telling her Marlene was in stable condition and out of intensive care. He finished by saying she should call him if she wanted more information.

NEXT TO THE LEWIS CHANNEL, YELLOWSTONE NATIONAL PARK, WYOMING

I wonder if that woman is dead. Why did she have to show up at the cabin in the first place? Her arrival started all this. Then that pompous professor. So typical of some college faculty. Think they are experts about everything and God's gift to the world. The fool thought he could trick me. Why couldn't he just go along and cooperate? Stupid. I had to stop him. I had no choice. What if there aren't any pieces of rock? What if there are rocks but they have no gold in them? What if this has been a wild goose chase? I've killed to get what I don't even know really exists. If there are so many pieces of rock and I can't carry them, then what will I do? I don't want to leave any behind. If there are pieces of rock and, hopefully, lots and lots of them with gold in them, I have to figure a way to carry them or if I can't carry them, I will have to hide them myself. Before leaving, I'm going to have to figure out how to place the blame for killing the professor away from me. *Maybe I shouldn't take any pieces of rock now. Leave them all where they are. Come back for them when everything blows over. I can come back then and take whatever there is. That's how I'll do it. They haven't been discovered for two hundred years so they can stay undiscovered a little while longer.*

SECURITY OFFICE, ADMINISTRATION BUILDING, HEADQUARTERS YELLOWSTONE NATIONAL PARK, MAMMOTH, MONTANA

His intercom buzzed. "Yes."

"Assistant Director Hoogstrate is on line one. I assume you want to take her call."

"You bet I do," replied Bruce Terpstra. "Hi, Alice. I assume you have more information about Marlene. More good news, I hope."

"You got it. I was able to talk with Marlene for a few minutes. She's gaining strength hourly. The doctors aren't saying for sure but they are hinting she will be able to leave the hospital in three or four days."

"That's great news. When you talked with her were you able to find out anything about the shooting?"

"Yes, but nothing I would call useful to our investigation, at least at this point. Marlene says she remembers walking onto the cabin porch and getting ready to knock on the door. She said she can't be sure about anything after that. I asked her to try hard to remember anything, even the slightest thing. She said she was sorry but she couldn't remember much else. She was quickly running out of energy by then and was mumbling more than forming words. I thought I heard her say, or mumble is more like it, a word, or it sounded like a word."

"What do you think you heard?"

I hesitate to even mention it. I can't be sure I heard correctly. I thought I heard her mumble the word, woman. Again, I could easily be wrong. I can't be sure. Not at all. She was fading fast. Plus, she's full of medication. Before I say for sure that's the word I heard, I want to talk with her again. I might be able to talk with her again in a few hours assuming the doctors and nurses allow it. Then I'll ask her to repeat what she said."

"When you heard her say what you think you heard, what were the two of you talking about?"

"Bruce, I said I think I heard her mumble the word woman. Maybe she did. Maybe she didn't. When I talk with her again, I'll try to learn if she did say it. If she did, I'll try to have her tell me what she meant. At the time I heard her mumble, we were talking about the shooting and what she remembered."

"Fair enough. I don't mean to press you. It's just that we need to solve this shooting. Marlene needs justice done. We need to reassure our employees and visitors that we don't have a criminal running around Yellowstone prone to shooting people."

"I didn't think you were pressing, Bruce. After I talk with Marlene again, I'll let you know what I learn."

Placing the phone into its holder, he stared at a Yellowstone poster on the wall opposite his desk. *Was Marlene trying to communicate to Alice something about the shooting which involved a woman? I think there was at least one woman in the cabin, maybe two. Was the woman trying to warn Marlene? Could the shooter be a woman? Was a third woman involved?"*

ROAD BETWEEN GRANT VILLAGE AND THE SOUTH ENTRANCE YELLOWSTONE NATIONAL PARK, WYOMING

"This might be a total bust," said Parker. "Just because there was no specific mention of Lewis Lake, Lewis River, or Lewis Falls in those materials in the cabin, there is no guarantee Gretchen might have headed there. I know there isn't a lake near there but maybe she headed to the Fall River and the Fall River Falls area. Maybe somewhere else in that same area. We also don't know if she left the cabin, like Liz did, before the shooting or if she was there when the shooting occurred. If she was there, who knows where she is now."

"I know what you're saying but we have no other clue," responded Beth, "so we might as well check the Lewis areas first. What scares me is there have been two shootings, one a murder and the other, I pray, not a murder. Gretchen may somehow be involved in both. I have no idea how she might be involved but I'm scared she may be." Reaching into the pocket of her jacket, she pulled out her mobile phone and handed it to Parker. "I need to check if there is a text or voice message from Bruce. He told me he would keep me informed about Marlene VanderBrink. He should have more information by now about her condition. I do so hope it is good news. I don't want to check my phone while I'm driving so would you please check."

Taking the phone from Beth, Parker replied, "You have a voice message."

"Okay, I'm going to pull over and listen to it."

ALONG THE LEWIS CHANNEL BETWEEN SHOSHONE AND LEWIS LAKES YELLOWSTONE NATIONAL PARK, WYOMING

Is this the area I think the sketch was describing? Am I close to where the pieces of rock may be hidden? The sketch is imprecise, that is one matter which concerns me. Another is that this may be the wrong area. What should I expect from a Crow chief? I'm sure he knew what he was sketching but how am I supposed to read his mind some two hundred years later? I bet the Crow chief buried the pieces of rock in the ground or in between boulders, probably in crevices and then covered them. I might have to dig to get at them or get them out. If there aren't pieces of rock with gold in them, then what do I do?

"Thank goodness I've been in many of the more remote areas of Yellowstone including this one," said Beth. "I was here a couple of years ago with one of our wolf restoration teams. We located an alpha male and mating female here. Now there's a pack of about twelve wolves. At least that's what our wolf research team says. I know this general area is off limits to everyone. There is a den somewhere in this area. At this time of year, there are probably pups in the den. I realize we will be violating policy if we continue moving through this area but I'm willing to take the heat if we're caught. Can you believe I'm saying what I am? An official of Yellowstone saying it's okay to violate policy? Besides, I don't think the wolves will hold it against us if we don't bother them, if we even happen to get near where their den is located."

"No question about it, you sure do know your Yellowstone backcountry," said Parker. "Places like this are not seen by many people other than Yellowstone rangers, wildlife folk, and the few people who want to fish in the backcountry. You have to know how to follow a slightly used trail to find places like this. A good GPS unit is a must. You also have to know what your're doing to navigate through these fallen trees and rock areas. I'll say I'm glad you have your satellite phone with you. There isn't any network connection or cell phone service out here, I'm sure about that. We're quite a distance from any road. I had no idea there were such extensive meadows around here. If it wasn't for a wolf den being somewhere around here, this would be a great place to camp. Given what we are doing, I'd say it's okay to continue to move around in this area. If we get too close to the wolf den, wherever it is, I'm sure the wolves will let us know. Then we hightail it. But for now, let's keep going."

Smiling as she responded, she said, "Okay, I'll blame it on you if we are apprehended. It will be your fault and I won't be able to cover for you."

"Thanks a whole lot." Looking around, he continued, "I must say I think you were correct when you thought this place would be ideal for a Crow village. Are you sure you don't have some Native American blood infused with instincts for where a Crow chief would establish a village? Look what's here and very close by. Obviously elk and bison would be plentiful given the grasses and water nearby. Fish in either Lewis or Shoshone Lakes would be plentiful. I, for one, can verify there are plenty of trout in the Lewis Channel and also Lewis River. Then you have the rock wall on the side of the meadow, what looks like a small canyon at the far end of this meadow, and the Lewis Channel on the third side leaving only one side to defend. Access to food and the ability to defend the village from war parties were the two most important priorities for Native American tribes and both are here."

"This is a very large meadow but I have a particular place in mind near where the Channel enters Lewis Lake," replied Beth. "If I'm correct and it was once the location of a Native American village, it doesn't at all mean it was Swift Eagle's village." Laughing, she continued, "It would be like winning the lottery if I guessed correctly and the place I have in mind was where Swift Eagle located his village. There's no way to tell if a village was even around here let alone know it was Swift Eagle's unless some group or historical agency did some heavy duty excavation and archaeological work around here. You're correct. It's an ideal place for obtaining food and water while being an easily defended location."

"So, let's go on the assumption this meadow is where Swift Eagle once established his village. If he did discover pieces of rock with gold in them, let's also assume he would hide them in a remote place which he could get close to on horseback. Of course, not too far from his village would also be important but not as important as a remote place. I know, two huge assumptions, but we have to start somewhere. With all the elk and bison that would be feeding on this meadow grass, hunting parties wouldn't have to travel far. Assuming Swift Eagle didn't go with groups of warriors to scout for signs of enemy tribes, he wouldn't have gone much of a distance from this location. If the gold he allegedly hid was in small pieces of rock, he would have been able to hide them anywhere; in the ground, behind or underneath larger rocks mixed in with other small rocks, who knows where? The question for us right now is what direction from the village and how far do we think Swift Eagle would have ventured to hide the pieces of rock. If we figure that out, we may be close to locating Gretchen."

Laughing, she responded, "Talk about assumptions. Those are some whoppers. But, I don't have anything better to guide us, so I'll take your assumptions and run with them."

"Thanks a whole lot for nothing."

"Oh come on. You can take it. You're a big boy. And, I'm giving you a compliment for a change. You're getting better at this outdoor stuff besides guiding a float boat down a river or standing in a river or stream helping somewhere cast a fly. When I think back to when you first arrived in Montana, you were a real greenhorn. A snobby easterner is what we thought of all of you eastern U.S. types."

"What did you expect? Mr REI? Massachusetts isn't what you would call the outdoor adventure capital of the U.S. But, thanks anyway."

Kneeling on the ground and opening the topo map, she pointed to a place on it as she spoke, "We're here by the Lewis Channel. Notice the several streams and creeks in the area. If we're going to check each one for a sign that Gretchen may have followed one of them, assuming she is following the sketch Liz referred to in those papers she left in the cabin, we have long hours ahead of us with very little chance at being successful."

"Let's not start out being defeated," replied Parker. "Who knows, we may be lucky and find a clue which tells us Gretchen was here. We need to start somewhere and keep going until we find her." Handing his binoculars to Beth, he pointed in a direction paralleling Lewis Channel. "Take a look. Do you see those circling birds? They look to me to be vultures. If they are, there's something drawing their attention. I'm not being an alarmist, but we should check what it is that's drawing their attention."

Holding the binoculars to her eyes, she responded, "Yes, I see them. I agree. Those are vultures. Probably an elk carcass. Maybe what's remaining from a kill by the resident wolfpack. I just thought of something. It would be an added bonus if we discovered the den of the wolfpack while also finding Gretchen. That would really be cool. As for those vultures, I don't even want to think there's a body out there. But, you are right. We do need to check." Handing the binoculars to him, she knelt again and looked at the topo map on the ground. "One of the areas we need to check is in that direction so we will be killing two birds with one stone, pardon the pun." Standing, she folded the map and placed in into her backpack. "We might as well get going. I'm trying to keep myself thinking positively."

ALONG A STREAM, EAST OF THE LEWIS CHANNEL, YELLOWSTONE NATIONAL PARK, WYOMING

Pointing toward a stand of lodgepole pine trees on a rocky hillside about one hundred fifty yards from the Lewis Channel, Parker said, "Whatever has attracted those vultures is in those trees on that hillside."

Walking with Parker toward the trees to which he had pointed, Beth felt her anxiety increase as her breathing became more labored. *What if there's a body? What if it's Gretchen? I know it's a long shot there's a body instead of an animal's carcass, but I can't shake the feeling of dread. My gut tells me this isn't going to be good. I have to be prepared for the worst.* Walking together as they came closer to the trees, several vultures rose into the air, their wings slapping, protesting the disturbance Beth and Parker were causing. Entering the trees, Parker allowed Beth to walk in front of him. He almost smacked into her backside when she stopped quickly. He heard a sharp intake of air from her along with a gasp. Looking over her shoulder, he saw what had caused her to stop. It wasn't an animal carcass. Animals don't wear clothes. Unless his eyes were deceiving him, before them, several yards away, was a body. He felt Beth sag into him. He put his arms around her thinking she might collapse. "Oh no, no," she gasped into his chest. "It can't be. It can't be."

Hugging her, he felt her shaking and breathing unevenly. *I can't allow her to lose control and breakdown. I have to take charge.* "Beth, stay here. I'll go look at the body. Please, stay here." Still holding onto him, he felt here shaking and her voice was little more than a whisper.

"Is it Gretchen? I can't look. I'm so scared it's Gretchen."

Slowly, he led her to a flat-top, knee-high boulder. "Sit here. We don't know anything about the body so let's not jump to conclusions. We don't know that it's Gretchen. Let me go and see who it is. It's probably a visitor who had a heart attack. You know it happens periodically in Yellowstone. You said you were feeling positive. Let's keep it that way." Making sure she was breathing more normally and, from what he could tell, more her usual self, he walked toward where a few vultures had returned while Beth and he had been by the boulder. As he neared the body, the vultures flew off providing a clearer view. Pieces of clothing lay scattered, having been ripped by the sharp beaks of the vultures. Stealing himself against what he anticipated seeing, he walked to the body.

ALONG THE LEWIS CHANNEL, YELLOWSTONE NATIONAL PARK, WYOMING

Once the feelings of surprise and relief had left him, Parker knelt down next to the body. Without a doubt, it was a male. The vultures and possibly other scavengers had begun to do their thing but not enough to leave any doubt the body was that of a young man. The victim's shirt was a bloody mess which Parker suspected meant he'd been shot. *Given Beth's frame of mind, I don't want her to see this even though she's probably seen worse. I know she's seen a person mauled by a grizzly and people injured in terrible car accidents. A lot more gruesome than this. She does need to know the body isn't Gretchen.* Jogging back to where she was still seated on the boulder, clutching her knees to her chest, he took her into his arms and said in as gentle a voice as he could muster, "It isn't Gretchen. It's a young male." He heard her begin to cry which quickly turned into sobs. Pulling her to him, he held her tightly. "It's okay, Beth. It's okay." He knew the sobs were those of relief. A loosening of the dam of built-up worry and anxiety.

"I was so scared," she said as the sobbing gave way to staggered breaths. "When I thought it was Gretchen, I felt so guilty. First Marlene, then Boersma, then Gretchen, and all because of my making Marlene go check on Gretchen. Oh, Parker, what have I done?"

In as comforting a tone of voice as he could muster, he replied, "You haven't done anything. None of this is your fault. You didn't kill anyone or cause anyone to be shot. Somebody is doing this for some reason which we don't know. We don't even know if Gretchen is involved. What we need to do is continue to search for her after we contact Bruce. I need someone from Security to help me. The victim needs to be identified and the area needs to be investigated. The body needs to be moved but not until after a medical examiner checks for cause of death. Bruce, and I suppose Janet, will eventually need to decide about how to proceed."

Her breathing back to normal, she responded, "You're right. We need to follow proper protocol. Who should we contact first, Bruce or Janet?"

"Good question. I was thinking that you should contact Bruce first. Let him go from there and contact Janet. It's going to be a while before a medical examiner can get here. Your security people can get here faster than anyone Janet can send. Bruce will certainly respond to a call from you. I'm all for leaving Janet out of this for as long as possible. Until the cause of death is determined, the death won't be an investigation for Janet until it's ruled a homicide. So, let Bruce contact Janet if he so chooses."

"I know you two want to get going," said Bruce. "I don't think you need to stay here any longer. I have your statements. The assistant medical examiner won't be here for a while so Delores will stay here until the scene is all wrapped up." Delores Gelderloos was the Yellowstone supervisory ranger for the Southeast region of Yellowstone. She had been called by Bruce who had arrived about an hour earlier after Beth had contacted him, explained the situation, and given him the location where she and Parker had found the body.

"So do you suspect foul play, Bruce?" asked Parker.

"I'm not a medical examiner but I've been around shootings and this looks like a homicide to me. I didn't see any bullet casings. Determining the type and caliber of gun might be difficult unless there is a bullet lodged somewhere in him or on the ground somewhere near the body."

"Another thing," replied Beth. "You said there's no backpack or any evidence of this guy being a hiker or camper. No fishing equipment either. So what was he doing out here? If he had taken out a backcountry permit, we might be able to find out who he is by accessing the BackCountry Permit Data Base and looking through the permits registered over the past several days for campers going into this area. But, then again, maybe he didn't register."

"Bruce, we didn't contact Janet," said Parker. "We thought you should decide if you wanted to alert her to the probability of another homicide in Yellowstone."

"I'm not going to contact Janet, at least not yet. I'll decide later after the assistant medical examiner tells me her determination."

Turning to face both Bruce and Parker, Beth said, "Let's not waste anymore time. We need to get going, Parker, and let Bruce deal with Janet, if he so chooses. Until we know who this guy is and how he died, we are only speculating which doesn't at all help in finding Gretchen. If you want to engage in speculation, let me add another possibility. Maybe this guy was another victim of whoever shot Marlene and killed the Boersma fellow. Gretchen may be with this murderer and she is probably being held against her will."

"Okay, Beth. Let's get our things together and get going. If we are lucky, we will find some evidence we are on the right track and hopefully close to locating Gretchen."

Shouldering their backpacks, they told Bruce to keep them informed if and when he learned anything useful. In particular, Beth asked him to let her know the latest about Marlene and how her recovery was progressing.

Foolish. Dumb. Stupid. Trying to overpower me. I said over and over don't try to trick or overpower me. Why didn't either of them believe me? I told them once we found Swift Eagle's pieces of rock we would share them. Generous of me but instead, each of them tried something stupid. All I want is to find that gold. I didn't want to kill anyone but what choice did I have?

They made the choice for me. Now it's only me. I have to be smart. Let me think. I got it. I need to be a victim. That's it. I'll shoot myself and say I was shot trying to escape. I know enough from my college anatomy class that if I shoot myself through the fatty portion of my thing, I won't bleed too badly. I can use the bandage and tape from the safety kit in my backpack to fashion a bandage. That should work. Thank goodness I grabbed the backpack before getting away from the cabin. My leg will hurt but I can manage. I hope no grizzly picks up the scent of the blood. That's all I need. A grizzly with which to contend. No thanks. Now, what else do I need to do to cover my story? On TV, the weapon is always important in any investigation. No weapon really messes up an investigation. That's what I'll do. Get rid of the gun. Throw it in the Channel. The current will carry it quite far away even though it weighs more than I would like it to. The current in the Channel is strong enough, I believe, to move it along. Okay, what else do I need to do? Think. The gun's gone. There's no witnesses. I've been shot. What am I missing? I'm good. After I shoot myself in my thigh, I need to move away from here and give the impression I was running away after I was shot. I need to leave a blood trail. Okay, I'm ready. Here goes."

"Did you hear that? It sounded like a shot." shouted Beth.

"Yeah, I heard something. Not sure it was a shot. It might have been a tree or two falling and hitting the ground. What do you think?", replied Parker.

"There. Another one," shouted Beth.

"I think you're right. "I don't think those were trees falling. Trees make more of a crashing sound. I've been at the practice range many times and heard gunshots. Those were two shots. I'm betting on it." Pointing in a direction across the meadow from them where the Lewis Channel make a turn and came close to a side of the meadow and a large number of rocks and shrubbery existed, she continued, "I think they came from that direction. You think so too?"

"Yeah, I think you're right. Somewhere across the meadow near the Channel." Pointing toward where numerous rocks dotted the landscape, he continued, "It sounded like it was in the vicinity of those rocks up ahead. Sound travels so well out here because there aren't any other noises. Those shots could have come from quite a distance. I couldn't tell how far away but I don't think too far away."

"I agree. I feel we may be closer than we think," said Beth. "Even if they came from closer by, there still is a lot of territory across this meadow between us and where they might have come from. We need to find out what those shots were all about as quickly as we can. I don't like this at all. Gretchen may be in trouble for all we know."

"Don't jump to conclusions. The shots probably don't have anything to do with Gretchen," replied Parker. "I say we keep going along the Channel toward where we think those shots came from. Even though there isn't a trail, it makes the most sense for anyone hiking in this area to follow the Channel."

"Okay, I won't think the worst. I'll be positive and believe Gretchen isn't anywhere near those shots. You may be right, but I still think with so much territory to cover, we need to also look away from the Channel. Tell you what. You continue to stay near the Channel. I'll be about one hundred yards or so from you. Between you and the Channel."

Parker didn't like the idea of her being by herself even if she wasn't going to be that far away. If what they heard were indeed shots, someone was out there with a gun. That could mean real trouble. *Better to stay together. I need to be close enough to immediately help her if needed.* "I'm quite sure there is someone out there with a gun. We should stay close to each other in case one of us needs help dealing with a hostile situation. Let's not separate. Let's stay together."

"We simply can't cover enough territory if we stick together. We can get to the other person quickly if we need to. I'm going to only be a short distance away. Let's not waste time arguing about this. How about every five minutes we check in with each other. Since we aren't able to text, just yell as loudly as you can. Sound travels far here. We won't have any trouble hearing each other."

"You know I don't like it but I also know you won't change your mind. Okay, every five minutes yell as loudly as you can. No shout means come quickly. Don't forget."

"See how we can agree without any hard feelings? It's one of the many things I like so much about you." Looking at her watch, she continued, "We shout to each other in five minute intervals. No exceptions. Every five minutes"

"Okay. Every five minutes. No exceptions."

ALONG THE LEWIS CHANNEL, YELLOWSTONE NATIONAL PARK, WYOMING

She knew Parker didn't want them to separate. She appreciated his concern for her safety. She also knew he was concerned about her in general even though she had shown him several times she could take care of herself. He certainly wasn't a chauvinist. His concern for her was genuine. It was another example of his feelings for her. She knew he cared for her as she did for him. *Why haven't our feelings for each other blossomed into a deeper and more intimate relationship? Is he waiting for a signal from me? Should I make an overt move? Would I drive him away if I did?* She brought her thoughts back to the shots. No mistaking it. Gun shots not too far away. Two gun shots within the last several minutes. *What is going on? Is there a poacher at work slaughtering elk? Maybe more than one poacher? If not a poacher, could someone have been shot? Killed? It can't be Gretchen! No. No. It can't be Gretchen! The shots sounded like they came from straight ahead.* She shouted at the top of her lungs just as she heard his shouting. Jogging in the direction of the sound of the shots, she thought she saw a person in the distance fall to the ground. *What did I just see? Is that a person? If it is, why did the person fall down? Did we hear this person being shot?*

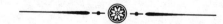

I can't believe this. What's she doing here? How did she find me? Now I have to deal with her too. What can I do to throw her off? Has she seen the body? I should have tried to hide it but how would I know someone was so close? If she saw it, will she draw the conclusion I need her to make? There aren't any witnesses. My story can't be contradicted by anyone. What's the best way to make sure I'm a victim? Maybe I should let her find me so I can tell her my story. Yes, that's the way to go. If I try to run and she sees me, she will wonder why I'm running away from someone who can rescue me. I need her to find me. I'll tell her my story. She has no choice but to believe me. Especially when she sees my leg wound. I'll tell her it was fortunate that I escaped even though I was shot in my thigh. It's my word against a dead man. I'll start groaning when she gets closer. Claim I was running away and was shot, collapsed, and hit my head. I have to pull off a real acting job.

"Gretchen! Gretchen!" Beth shouted Gretchen's name as she ran toward where Gretchen was lying on the ground. As she drew closer to her, she heard her groan as she tried to stand to meet Beth. *Oh dear God. What has happened? Is Gretchen hurt? I heard her groaning. She doesn't seem able to stand.* Running to Gretchen and reaching down to aid her, Beth said, "Gretchen, are you okay? Take it easy. You're hurt. Have you been shot? Let me take a look." *I need to get Parker here. He has that small medical kit.* "Parker! Parker! I need your help!"

"Aunt Beth, I'm so happy to see you. It has been a nightmare," responded Gretchen in a weak voice. "I got shot in my leg."

Beth could see the blood on Gretchen's lower left pant leg. "Hold on. Let me take a look at your leg." As gently as she could, she undid the belt of Gretchen's pants and lowered them. The bloody area of her left thigh was clearly visible. The wound didn't look too bad, at least Beth didn't think it was bleeding too profusely. Gretchen must have applied the bandage to the wound but it hadn't stopping the bleeding, only slowed it down. Beth knew she needed to try and slow the bleeding even more. *Where is Parker? Why hasn't he responded? I need him.*

"Aunt Beth, after he shot me I wanted to get away from him even though he was shot too. He may be dead. I stumbled and fell down. I think I hit my head. I must have been knocked out for a few minutes. Thank goodness you arrived." Grimacing, she tried to continue but she began to sob and the tears flowed freely.

"Everything is okay now. I'm going to look more closely at your wound. Grit your teeth. Scream if you have to." Removing the bandage, Beth was able to look more closely at the wound. She could see the bullet had passed through Gretchen's thigh and hadn't hit any major arteries or veins. Taking off her blouse, she used it as a makeshift tourniquet. Tying it as tightly as she could, she could see the bleeding tapering off. "There. I think that will slow the bleeding even more. You stay here. Lean against that boulder. Put your leg up on this rock if you can." Moving a small rock, she placed it under Gretchen's foot. *Parker. Where are you? We need you.*

"He shot me, Aunt Beth. He also shot the professor. It was awful! I was so scared! He also shot a woman who came to our cabin. It's been terrible. He said he wanted to find the pieces of rock with gold in them that Liz had told him about which she believed had been hidden by an Indian chief. He made us go with him. He said if we cooperated and helped him find the gold, he would share it with us. He said he wouldn't harm us. He lied."

"Gretchen, just rest now. I'm going to contact Bruce Terpstra and request a helicopter to take you for proper medical attention. You can tell Bruce all about what happened when you're with him in the helicopter. You need medical attention." Shouting, she yelled, "Parker! Parker! Where are you? Come quickly!"

ALONG THE LEWIS CHANNEL, YELLOWSTONE NATIONAL PARK, WYOMING

Shouting her name and jogging toward where he thought she would be, Parker said, "Beth. Beth. Okay, I hear you. I will be there as soon as possible." After no more than ten or fifteen seconds, he came next to her. "Thank goodness you are okay." Seeing Gretchen with what looked like a bloodied shirt or blouse wrapped around her thigh while her leg rested on a boulder, he said, "Gretchen, are your okay?"

"As you can see," said Beth, she's been wounded. Thank goodness, the bullet passed through the fleshy portion of her thigh. The wound looks worse than it is, at least that's how it looks to me."

"That's good news." Looking back toward where the man's body was, Parker said, "We must make sure we don't touch anything. This whole area is likely a crime scene. We may have another homicide." Kneeling next to Gretchen, he continued, "Did you know how that man back there died?" Before Gretchen answered, he said to Beth, "We need to get Bruce here as quickly as he can make it. I'll also contact Janet. This is too much for me to handle."

Pulling Parker aside, after she told Gretchen she and Parker needed to contact Bruce and the FBI, she said, "There is something strange here. It doesn't add up. I can't get my mind around a dead man and Gretchen wounded. Doesn't it seem strange to you too?"

"What do you mean strange? Strange in what way?"

"I've only given this a cursory thought. It doesn't add up for me. I'm confused. But, I don't want to influence or bias you. You need to analyze this yourself. Right now, you are the FBI at the site of a probable homicide. You need to act as an FBI agent would. We also need to have Bruce look it over. When he comes, I want him to bring his gun powder residue and gun powder burn test kits with him. He needs to do those tests as soon as possible. The results would help me sort out my thinking."

"What do you mean, something doesn't add up? What something? What's confusing to you? What do you suspect? Why the test kits?"

"I'll explain later. As I said, I don't want to prejudice your perspective. Just try to recreate what your logic tells you happened here. While you do that, I'm going to contact Bruce. You contact Janet." Taking the satellite phone she carried for emergency purposes, she called Bruce's mobile number. After three rings, Bruce answered, "Hello, this is Bruce Terpstra."

"Hi, Bruce. It's Beth. I'm not going to explain or give you details, but there is a man's body near Lewis Channel. It looks to me to be a homicide. Parker is with me. He's contacting Janet VanKampen. We found my niece. She's been shot. Thankfully, it's not a serious wound. The bullet passed through the fleshy portion of her thigh. The bleeding is controlled but she needs to have medical attention. Can you send a helicopter to take her to Jackson?"

"Beth, please tell me you're kidding. Another homicide in Yellowstone on top of the other one. This just can't be."

"Sorry, Bruce, I'm deadly serious. Excuse the pun. As I said, Parker is with me. He's been deputized by Janet but he and I both feel you should lead on this situation, at least until some official FBI agents take over. Parker doesn't feel competent enough to conduct an investigation involving a probable homicide. How soon can you get here? If you need approval for the helicopter, I'm authorizing it. We also need a medical examiner. You and the medical examiner can come together."

"Are you sure your niece only has a superficial wound?"

"Yes, As I said, the bullet passed through the fleshy portion of her thigh. I tied a makeshift tourniquet and the bleeding, which wasn't bad to begin with, is minor now. One more thing, Bruce. Something very important. Please bring your gun powder residue and gun powder burn kits. Don't forget them."

"Why, Beth? Is there something you think needs to be done? I haven't conducted those tests in a long time. I'm not sure I remember all the proper procedures. The kits are old. The results might not be valid."

"Let's just say, Bruce, I want to make sure about something. I understand your reluctance, given that conducting those tests isn't something you do regularly, but you're the best we have. I'm not going to say anything more. I want you to be totally open to possibilities without any bias from me."

"Okay, if you feel it's important and necessary, I'll take your advice. I'll commandeer the helicopter. I'll have Margaret Lagerway come along. She can take care of your niece. What about the body? What can you tell me about it?"

"Parker and I believe he hasn't been dead very long. Perhaps no more than one-half hour or so. We think he was shot once. No sign of a struggle. No backpacks or camping gear. I have no idea who he is. Gretchen says he shot her."

"What a mess. Thanks goodness you are out in the boonies. No reporters. No media. Let's try and keep a lid on this for as long as we can. I'll be there as quickly as I can."

ALONG THE LEWIS CHANNEL, YELLOWSTONE NATIONAL PARK, WYOMING

"Janet, it's Parker. I'm using a satellite phone so our connection should be okay. I'm in Yellowstone along the Lewis Channel. I hate to tell you but there is another body. First impression is it's a homicide. Bruce Terpstra is on his way. I feel inadequate and ill-equipped to deal with another homicides on top of the one I'm already investigating. The male victim here could be the shooter of Marlene and Boersma. If I'm right, the homicide you're having me investigate is solved. I don't want to screw up this other one. I'm afraid I might. Is there an agent you can send? Maybe two? The more agents the better."

"Parker, you can't be serious. Another homicide! What is going on in Yellowstone? Three shootings and two homicides. There haven't been three shootings in Yellowstone in even one entire year ever since Teddy Roosevelt established the place. What's behind this outbreak of shootings? Is the area secure? You're fairly confident the shooter is dead?"

"It's only a guess on my part but I'll tell you why I think the way I do. Beth and I found some materials in the cabin where her niece was living which led us to believe Gretchen's roommate discovered something potentially very valuable. The shooter, whoever the person is or was, found out about this valuable something and went after it, wounding Marlene and killing Boersma, who somehow got in his way. We think he also shot Gretchen. wounding her superficially. He died

138

from a gunshot. How that happened is a mystery which your agents are going to have to figure out. Better qualified and experienced agents than me. Bottom line, I need help. The sooner, the better."

"If the shooter is dead from a gunshot, who shot him? Another shooter who may still be around there?"

"As I said, I would only be guessing so it isn't worth spending time talking about something which is only a guess. What's important are Gretchen and the body. How do you want to handle all this? As I said, Bruce is on the way. He is bringing Margaret Lagerway with him, at least I hope he is. She can do a preliminary examination of the body. She can also attend to Gretchen. I intend to turn over the scene to Bruce, unless you tell me differently. Again, I don't feel equipped to handle multiple homicides. Please get some agents here pronto."

"You said Bruce will be there soon. He certainly is equipped to assist you in conducting a preliminary investigation. Have him contact me so I will know what he thinks. I'll then decide how to proceed. If push comes to shove, I'll have to tell Carrie and Alex to leave Sandpoint. I hope it doesn't come to that but until Bruce can do his thing, as well as Margaret, I don't want to overreact. Remember, you are the FBI's representative. You carry the mantle of the FBI, at least until Carrie and Alex, or some other agents, take over."

Realizing his involvement wasn't going to change until FBI agents arrived, Parker said he would stay involved until at least an official FBI agent arrived.

"I contacted Bruce," said Beth. "He's on his way. He's using a helicopter. Margaret Lagerway is with him. She will be able to treat Gretchen and make sure her condition is stable and there is nothing critical. There may be a medical examiner as well."

Beth and Parker were standing at one end of a small meadow where the terrain changed to a rocky, uneven surface with shrubs and smaller pine trees giving way to a hillside covered with rocks, shrubs, and large pine trees. The Lewis Channel was only a few yards from where they stood and the sound of water rushing over the boulder strewn Channel meant they had to shout to hear each other. Turning toward the other end of the meadow, Beth said, "I hear a helicopter now. That must be Bruce. It'll have to land a little way from here. I'll make sure he can see me as soon as he lands."

Responding in a loud voice, Parker said, "I hear it too. You go meet Bruce. I'm sure he has questions. You can answer them and prepare him for what he is going to find. I'm going to talk with Gretchen for a few minutes. She must be wondering what's going on." Walking to where Gretchen was sitting on the ground with her back against a boulder, he knelt down next to her. "How are you feeling? Much pain? A medical person will soon be here. If need be, you can be airlifted by helicopter. Do you feel up to telling me what happened?"

"Oh, Parker, it was terrible! Ever since Aaron shot that woman at the cabin I've been so terrified. He kidnapped Boersma and me and then shot him. He tried to kill me too but I was fortunate I was able to get away from him before he shot me. I think after he shot me he shot himself. He must have known he wasn't going to get away with what he had done. If he didn't shoot himself, then there must be another killer around here."

"Why did he bring you here? Did he say what he was after? Killing Professor Boersma for what reason?"

"Liz believed she had discovered where a Crow chief had hidden some pieces of rock with gold in them. Somehow, Aaron learned about what Liz thought she had discovered. I think Liz and he dated a couple of times. She never mentioned him to me so I was surprised when he showed up at the cabin. He had a gun. After he shot that woman at the cabin he became almost fanatical. He told Boersma and me we were going to help him find the pieces of rock and once we did find them, we would share them. Of course, we didn't believe him. I just wanted to get away! Boersma and Aaron got into a huge argument over the gold. That is when Aaron shot him. He then told me he would do the same to me if I didn't cooperate. He knew that Liz knew the most about the possible location of the pieces of rock so I guess he thought she told me where they were hidden." Her body began to tremble and she began to sob. Parker could hardly understand her as she tried talking between sobs. "The entire time I was terrified. I wanted to get the gun away from him but I was too scared."

ALONG THE LEWIS CHANNEL, YELLOWSTONE NATIONAL PARK, WYOMING

The helicopter had landed in the far end of the meadow. Beth jogged to it and saw Bruce descend from the side door of the chopper. Parker was with Gretchen on the other end of the meadow. Bruce was followed by Margaret Lagerway. A third person, a woman whom Beth didn't recognize but whom she assumed was a medical examiner, joined them as she continued to jog toward them. Parker saw Bruce, Margaret, and the other woman, who was carrying a large black briefcase type of bag, which he assumed was a medical bag, greet Beth. All four walked quickly to where Gretchen and Parker were waiting. Immediately, the woman, who had introduced herself as Wilma Vogelzang, knelt down next to Gretchen and began examining her thigh.

"You're lucky, the wound is superficial. The tourniquet certainly helped." Looking up at Beth, she continued, "Good move on your part. Your quick thinking and action helped slow down the bleeding." Turning back to speak to Gretchen she continued, "I want to give you a couple of shots of pain killer and some antibiotics. Then I'll clean the wound and bandage it. Do you know if you are allergic to any anesthesia? How about antibiotics?"

"I've never had allergies. Thank you for helping me," responded Gretchen.

While Margaret, Wilma, and Beth stayed with Gretchen, Parker and Bruce walked to where the body still lay in the position Beth and Parker had found it. Using the gun powder residue and burn kits Beth told him to bring, Bruce dusted the fingers and palms of both hands of the body. Parker had never been this close to actual gun powder residue and burn tests so he didn't know if Bruce was conducting the tests correctly in accordance with proper procedures. "Bruce, not the best conditions to conduct tests, huh?"

"Certainly not. Unfortunately, not the most technically up-to-date equipment either. But it's what it is. I'll do the best I can and hope the results are meaningful. Once the body is in the morgue, a more careful examination can be done with up-to-date equipment." Parker continued to watch as Bruce withdrew a portable LED bright flashlight, with an attached magnifying lens, to examine each finger and the two palms. After conversing with each other, Bruce handed Parker the flashlight and told him to do the same thing. Walking back to Margaret, Wilma, and Beth, Bruce said, "Beth, I'd like to have Margaret and Wilma look at something curious about the victim. Would you stay with Gretchen and make sure she is comfortable while the three of us join Parker for a few minutes?"

"Sure, Bruce," responded Beth. "What are you curious about?"

"Curious might not be the proper word," said Bruce. "It may be nothing. "Margaret and Wilma, let's have you take a look. This shouldn't take long. We then will get Gretchen ready to be flown to the Jackson hospital."

Thinking about what Bruce had said, Beth thought to herself, "*I wonder what Bruce thinks is curious about the body? It seems obvious to me what happened. Gretchen told us what happened, so what might Bruce be thinking?*"

"Aunt Beth, my leg is starting to feel strange," said Gretchen. "I need to get to a hospital and have a doctor check it. I don't like the way it is feeling. When can we leave here?"

"Bruce said whatever he wants Margaret and Wilma to examine won't take long. You should be out of here shortly," replied Beth. "I suspect the pain medicine is kicking in. That's why your leg is feeling funny. Here come Margaret and Wilma now."

Walking up to Beth, Margaret said to her, "Bruce wants you to join Parker and he for a few minutes. Wilma and I will get Gretchen ready to be flown with us to the Jackson hospital."

Speaking to Gretchen, Beth said, "Gretchen, Margaret and Wilma will get you ready for the chopper. I'm going to join Parker and Bruce for a few minutes. Concentrate on conserving your strength. I'll be back shortly." Walking toward where Parker and Bruce were by the body, she saw Parker kneeling on one side of it and Bruce kneeling on the other side. *What are they looking at? I don't like the feeling I'm getting in my gut. Something's going on.*

Meeting her about ten yards from Bruce and the body, Parker said, "Beth, Bruce and I examined the body. We had Margaret and Wilma examine it as well. I don't want you to be surprised. We're having trouble making connections. We're questioning how he was shot."

"What's there to question? Gretchen told us what happened. This Aaron fellow shot Gretchen as she was running from him. None of us can know what was in his head but for some reason, known only to him, he decided to kill himself. End of story."

Knowing she would react with an unbelieving perspective, he was careful with his response. "I'd rather you hear directly from Bruce and not only from me." They then walked the few yards to where Bruce continued to kneel by the body. "Bruce, I'm now wearing my FBI hat. I want Beth to hear what preliminary conclusions you, Wilma, and Margaret have reached. I realize your conclusions are just that – preliminary - and might be changed once an autopsy is conducted and forensic analyses completed. Before that, Beth should be brought into the loop so she has the same picture we do. Please describe the preliminary conclusions all of you have reached."

The tone of Parker's voice triggered a feeling of dread in Beth. *What's with this FBI stance by him? Why all the drama? What is Parker unwilling to tell me? I don't like where this may be going.* Her thoughts were interrupted by Bruce. "Beth, when you contacted me, you told me to bring my gun powder residue and burn kits. Why did you want me to be sure I had them when I came?"

"I remembered something from a seminar I attended last year. You know the seminar we all attended about evidence not being compromised at a homicide scene where a gun had been used and the suspected shooter was present. I remember the emphasis regarding gun powder residue and powder burns being important pieces of evidence and that tests needed to be done before the crime scene and the individuals involved in the shooting might become compromised by the environment, like rain or decomposition due to humidity or intense sun. My asking you, Bruce, to have your gun powder residue and burn kits was a routine request. I didn't mean anything special by it."

"Well, I'm thankful you reminded me. I used both test kits as part of our examination of the body. I realized I'm not an expert in gun powder residue or powder burns so, as Parker said, our conclusions about what happened here and how this went down are preliminary. Any conclusions we reach will require verification. I believe I followed the proper protocols and procedures in conducting the tests. The kits are not up to date but I'm hoping the results are accurate anyway. Once the body is in the morgue, tests can be conducted again by the experts using the newest equipment. Again, I emphasize our conclusions are preliminary."

"I understand, Bruce," responded Beth. "What I don't understand is why you are being so insistent about my understanding your conclusions are preliminary. Nothing is ever totally conclusive until the autopsy and other tests are conducted in a proper setting. This situation isn't any different from others about preliminary and final conclusions."

Speaking to Parker, Bruce said, "Parker, please go and have Margaret and Wilma join Beth and me. You can stay with Gretchen. I think it's best to have Beth hear from Margaret and Wilma the results of their examination. I'll then piggyback with the results of my tests. You already know what are our preliminary conclusions are so you don't need to be here with us."

ALONG THE LEWIS CHANNEL, YELLOWSTONE NATIONAL PARK, WYOMING

My story worked. They don't seem to suspect me. I've watched enough CSI to know that without the weapon and with no witnesses, nothing or no one can contradict my story. All I need to do is stick to my story. No matter what anyone says or does to try and make me change my story, I have to stick with it. Aunt Beth believes me. She won't change her mind. She will protect me. My leg is really hurting. I should complain big time about it so that the security guy won't ask me too many questions. Here comes Parker. What does he want? I know he and Aunt Beth have a thing for each other. He probably believes me too since Aunt Beth does and he wouldn't want to go against her. These two medical women and the security guy are the problem. I need to get out of here and away from them. I'll insist that I leave now for the Jackson hospital. I need to be groaning when they get back here.

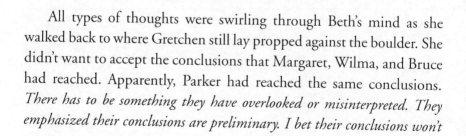

All types of thoughts were swirling through Beth's mind as she walked back to where Gretchen still lay propped against the boulder. She didn't want to accept the conclusions that Margaret, Wilma, and Bruce had reached. Apparently, Parker had reached the same conclusions. *There has to be something they have overlooked or misinterpreted. They emphasized their conclusions are preliminary. I bet their conclusions won't*

hold up once the forensic experts are able to do more extensive and in-depth investigations. I'm not criticizing any of them, but they aren't trained in forensic analysis like the experts are. I'm sure this will all be straightened out and quickly corrected once the experts undertake their work. As she neared Gretchen, Beth could hear her groaning. *Why isn't Parker doing something?* In a tone of voice which conveyed her annoyance she said, "Parker, don't you hear her groaning? She must be having significant pain. We need to get her to the Jackson hospital."

Pulling Beth aside so Gretchen would not hear him, he responded, "Yes, I hear her. We both know her wound isn't serious. She certainly has some pain but nothing intense. Margaret gave her pain medication which is probably not fully absorbed into her body. Now that you know what Margaret, Wilma, and Bruce concluded, we need to hear how Gretchen explains what they described to both of us." While Parker had been talking, Margaret, Wilma, and Bruce had joined them and now stood with them.

Directing her question to Margaret in a tone of voice conveying her impatience, Beth said, "My niece is obviously in pain. She says it is getting worse. She needs to get to a hospital. I'm not criticizing your treatment, but a more comprehensive examination by doctors is warranted. Let's get her to Jackson pronto."

"Your niece's level of pain can't be so intense that she can't focus and explain what we described to you," said Bruce. "What do you think, Margaret?"

"I injected a pain suppressing medication along with an antibiotic. Unless she has a very low tolerance for pain, she's experiencing the normal pain level associated with a wound of her type. I can give her some more pain medication if I'm convinced she needs it but I doubt I'll have to. In my judgment, she's more than capable of answering some questions before we load her into the chopper."

Gretchen's groaning intensified as they were talking. Speaking directly to her, Margaret asked, "Gretchen, are you having a great deal of pain?"

"Yes, it's become much worse. I need to get to a hospital. Can't we go now?"

"We can leave as soon as you clarify some matters which we're still having difficulty understanding," responded Bruce.

"I've already told you everything I can remember. I was so terrified that I'm surprised I remember as much as I do. I'm sorry if I can't remember too many details. How many times do I have to repeat the same things? Aaron shot everyone, including me as I was running away from him. He then must have shot himself. Maybe after I get treated at a hospital and the pain diminishes I will remember more."

Beth felt the others were holding back in their questioning out of respect for her and a reluctance to come on strongly and aggressively toward Gretchen in Beth's presence. She sensed she needed to take the lead and show the others she was with them in their approach to questioning Gretchen. *Just because Gretchen is my niece, I can't allow our relationship to cloud or prejudice my thinking.* "Gretchen, tell us as much as you remember. I know you've already told the story from the first shooting at the cabin until now, but please tell it again, trying to remember as much as you can. Don't skip anything, thinking it isn't important. Concentrate on details."

"Just remembering how terrified I was and how awful it was to see those people shot makes my anxiety level go off the chart. I'll try and concentrate but I might not make it all the way since it was so horrible."

"Before you start, Gretchen, I need you to know I'm representing the FBI and I'm authorized to act on behalf of the FBI," said Parker. "Since at least one homicide occurred, I'm obligated to give you your Miranda rights. Doing so doesn't imply anything about your involvement, guilt, innocence or any other aspect of what happened or how it happened. I'm also obligated to tell you you have the right to have a lawyer present."

"Why would I need a lawyer? I did nothing but be a victim. Don't you believe me when I tell you I'm as much a victim as the others except I'm still alive? Aunt Beth, you believe me, don't you?"

Before Beth could answer, Bruce said, "It isn't about believing or not believing you. Margaret and I need clarification on certain aspects of the what, when, and how of all that took place. Parker, please give Gretchen her Miranda rights."

Beth did all she could to not talk although it was increasingly difficult not to come on strong and tell all of them to accept Gretchen's story and stop playing detective. As she was contemplating if she should say anything, Parker gave Gretchen her Miranda rights. He then asked if she wanted a lawyer to be present. Laughing, she said, "I've no need of a lawyer. Besides, if I said I wanted a lawyer, what would you do? Wait for one to come? I might die from an infection in my leg by that time. Let's get on with this foolishness."

ALONG THE LEWIS CHANNEL, YELLOWSTONE NATIONAL PARK, WYOMING

As Gretchen described the events she remembered, which were again no different from what she had conveyed previously, Parker knew Margaret, Wilma, and Bruce were poised to ask her about several matters which, while not directly contradicting her description, certainly made her description suspect. His thoughts bounced between the questions he felt they were about to ask and how he thought Beth was assimilating what she was hearing from Gretchen. *This has to be tough for Beth. Gretchen is her niece. Beth went out of her way and pulled some strings for Gretchen. If what Margaret, Wilma, and Bruce believe happened, will Beth feel betrayed? How should I act with Beth? Comfort her? Express my regret for Gretchen's betrayal? But if they are wrong, and they might be, then Beth might see me as jumping to conclusions.*

He was drawn back to Gretchen's description when Bruce said, "A few points of clarification. You saw Aaron, that's his name, correct? You saw him shoot Professor Boersma, correct? As you were running away from him he shot you too, the bullet hitting you in your thigh, correct?"

"How many times must I tell you? Aaron shot the woman at the cabin and also the professor. He tried to kill me too."

"Okay. Aaron shot Professor Boersma and you. Funny thing. We haven't found a gun. Any idea where it might be? Especially if Aaron shot himself after shooting you, the gun should be next to his body, maybe even still in his hand."

"I know nothing about any of that. Maybe after shooting himself there were a few seconds before he collapsed when he could have thrown the gun somewhere. That's probably how he did it. I don't know. Why are you questioning me about a gun which I know nothing about?"

"Please, Gretchen, I realize you may know nothing about what we are asking you but two people are dead," Beth said. "You are the only witness to how they died. Knowing as much as possible about how they died is very important. You certainly understand that."

Parker could hear in Beth's voice indication of hesitancy and uncertainty. He decided he needed to take over from her so she wouldn't compromise herself and possibly the investigation. "There is no one else from whom we can seek clarification," said Parker. "As your aunt just said, there was no one else here, at least we didn't find any evidence of a third person being anywhere around here. You and the fellow you call Aaron were here. Now, he is dead and can't provide clarification. You're the only person who can. I know career FBI agents will be interviewing you in the near future. You're going to have to describe everything to them so consider what we are doing now as a practice session of sorts for you." As Parker was talking, the whomp-whomp-whomp sound of an approaching helicopter grew louder.

"I'll go signal the chopper where to land," said Margaret. "I'll make sure we bring back a stretcher for Gretchen. Also an IV bag."

"Before we take you to the chopper," said Bruce, "One more time. You said Aaron shot you as you were running away from him. Then you believe he shot himself. Do I have that right?"

"How else could it have happened?" answered Gretchen. "You said you don't believe there was another person, someone who would have shot Aaron. So, he had to shoot himself. Yeah, you have it right."

Parker saw a young man with a flight helmet and a one piece flight suit, whom he surmised was the chopper pilot, walking toward them. He was carrying a stretcher. Speaking directly to Gretchen, Parker said, "I'm confused. Aaron had to shoot a gun at least two times. That would mean at least two shell casings near his body. We found only one shell casing near the body, not two. The one casing was a few feet from him. We found a second casing very close to where Beth found you after, as you say, you were shot by Aaron, running from him. I trust you can see how your recollection of the shootings and the evidence provided by the shell casings don't jive."

"Are you saying I'm lying? I've told you what I remember. Maybe a gust of wind moved one of the shell casings near me. You know how gusty the wind can be in Yellowstone. How do I know how a shell casing ended up near me? What difference does it make? I'm telling the truth. That's all that matters."

The chopper pilot had joined them while Gretchen was talking. "I'm going to need someone to join me for the flight to Jackson. You decide who it will be." Kneeling next to Gretchen, he continued, "Miss, you can walk with me to the chopper if you feel up to it or you can be carried on the stretcher. Either way, once we are on the chopper, I'm going to give you an IV, maybe two. Don't worry, I'm certified to give IVs. I did it in Iraq and Afghanistan. Since the IVs will stay in awhile, are you left or right handed? I'll put them in the wrist area of your non-dominant hand."

"I'm right handed. I can probably walk okay but I do feel weak. Maybe a stretcher makes the most sense." Lying on the stretcher, Gretchen continued, "Aunt Beth, will you please come with me? I'd feel much better if there was someone I knew with me. You can also contact my Dad. He needs to know what happened and that I'm okay."

Beth looked at Parker and he looked at her. He knew what she was thinking and she him. He knew she wanted to accompany Gretchen. Beth was a blood relative. She understood the grilling Gretchen was going to be subject to once the medical folks at the Jackson hospital released her to the FBI. *I don't want Beth to go. The evidence tells me Gretchen is a killer. Beth can't do a thing to help Gretchen. I wouldn't put it past Gretchen to try something stupid which might hurt Beth.*

I know what he's thinking. He doesn't want me to go with Gretchen. All he sees is a killer and my being with a killer. He doesn't understand I'm a blood relative. She's like the daughter I never had. I owe it to my cousin to stay with her through thick and thin. Sure, it doesn't look good for her but until it's proven she did the shootings, I'm not going to abandon her.

"Bruce, either you or I need to stay here until the agents, whom Janet permanently assigns to this case, are physically here," said Parker. "If you want to go with Gretchen, I'll stay."

I know what he's doing. He's trying to have Bruce go so that I can't go because there isn't enough room on the chopper. Before Bruce could answer, she said, "Bruce, I'm going with Gretchen. She's my cousin's daughter. I feel a responsibility to be with her. I'm sure there are all kinds of important matters needing your attention besides this situation. Yellowstone doesn't shut down because we aren't in our roles. Security issues and problems happen twenty-four, seven. You need to get back to your other responsibilities. You can go with Margaret and Wilma back to headquarters."

Bruce caught the vibes between Beth and Parker. He wanted no part of being in the middle. Responding he said, "You're my boss. If I disobeyed, I would be insubordinate. Parker, I'm going to head back to headquarters. You need to stay here until Janet's agents arrive. What my boss decides to do is up to her."

Beth smiled inwardly and said to herself, *"Brilliant move, Bruce. I owe you one. Parker's trapped."*

Bruce really boxed me in with that response. This boss stuff is nonsense. He just said that to get out from between us. I still have one more way to get her off the chopper. "Okay, I'll stay here. Bruce, you and Margaret take off. Wilma can go with Gretchen. Beth can stay with me and after the FBI agents arrive, she and I will figure out a way to get to Jackson to join Gretchen."

With a tone of voice Parker had heard before whenever Beth was nearing the point of expressing frustration, she said, "We've no idea when FBI agents will arrive. Once they do, you'll have to brief them and explain the preliminary conclusions. That will involve showing them the photos of the shell casings, their location, and so forth. You'll have to do all that before we can leave. The agents will have to make arrangements for the body to be taken to Jackson, Bozeman, or Billings. That'll take time which will involve you as well. Remember, you're the FBI's representative here and can't leave until the other agents are fully briefed and take over. I'm not going to wait around while all that transpires. I'm going to go with Gretchen. Wilma can go with Margaret and Bruce."

Realizing he had lost the argument and not wishing to alienate her. he replied, "Okay. You go with Gretchen. Wilma can go with Margaret and Bruce. I'll stay and work with the FBI agents."

ALONG THE LEWIS CHANNEL, YELLOWSTONE NATIONAL PARK, WYOMING

"How long had the body been here?" asked Carrie DeLange.

"Blood hadn't totally congealed when Beth and I arrived," answered Parker. "Very few flies too. It took us only a few minutes, after we heard two shots to come upon the body. I've been here since then."

"No one touched or moved anything, correct? No movement of the body or anything else, correct?"

"What you're seeing is how we found it. The exception is the shell casings," responded Parker. "Bruce took photos of their locations. Then we placed them into an evidence bag which he took with him. Margaret Lagerway and Wilma Vogelzang examined the body. They also did an examination of entrance and exit wounds to get an idea about distance from the shooter to the victim. They analyzed the direction the victim and the shooter were facing. Bruce did gun powder residue and burn tests. Other than those activities, nothing else was done that I know about."

"You told us about the conclusions of those tests," said Alex. Turning to talk directly to Carrie, he continued, "Carrie, why don't you go talk with the woman who was also shot but survived. She's who everyone suspects is the shooter, correct?"

"Before doing that," said Carrie, "I want to take several photos of the body. I know he was shot but I should officially do photos. There will be a through examination once the body is at the morgue. We need to review the documentation about the location of the body, how it was lying on the ground, and the ground immediately around it. After identification is determined and next of kin notified, an autopsy will be done at the morgue."

"Okay Carrie. You stay and take the photos. I'll go and talk with this woman," said Alex. "Parker, you come with me."

"Sure," replied Parker.

They walked toward where Gretchen was being readied to be loaded onto the chopper. As they walked, Alex said, "You've said this woman is Assistant Superintendent Richardson's cousin's daughter. I understand Beth is Assistant Richardson's first name and she treats this woman like a daughter. I realize theirs is a blood relationship, so I will be sensitive to it. Do you think Beth will pose a problem if I come on strongly with her niece? Should I ask her to leave us and join Carrie? I intend to focus on what this woman witnessed and her own injury. She was shot in her leg, correct? And you did say her name is Gretchen?

"Yes. Gretchen was shot in the fleshy portion of her left thigh. Beth slowed the bleeding with a homemade tourniquet. Margaret gave her pain medication and antibiotics. I don't know if either of those might affect her memory," replied Parker. "Beth won't be a problem. She's a professional. Given what we concluded and explained to her, she won't compromise her desire that justice be done."

"I'm pleased to hear that," said Alex. Pointing to the helicopter, he continued, "The chopper pilot is getting ready to transport Gretchen to the Jackson hospital. We won't have another chance to interview her until after she's treated there. I'll cover what I need to now. Then I'll fill in any gaps when Carrie and I interview her again in Jackson. I appreciate what you are telling me about Beth. As for Gretchen's memory, I'll be able to tell if its been affected by the medications." Walking to where Beth and the pilot were preparing to take Gretchen to the chopper, Alex introduced himself and explained his and Carrie's role. He then listened, without interruption, as Gretchen described being shot and her belief Aaron shot himself. "You remember at least two shots, correct? One shot which wounded you. The other which you believe was self inflicted. You didn't see him shoot either you or himself. Do I have this correct?"

"Yes, you do," responded Gretchen. "I don't know why I have to keep repeating over and over again the same things. My leg is really hurting. I need more pain medication. Aunt Beth, please help me."

Alex and Parker both looked at Beth wondering if she would respond. Parker could see Beth struggling. When she did, Parker knew his opinion of her professionalism was right on. Speaking directly to Gretchen, in a forceful tone of voice, she said, "Gretchen, it's critical this FBI agent has a complete understanding of how Aaron was killed and how you were shot. Your wound might be painful but it isn't life threatening. There won't be any long term effects, so it isn't necessary to take you to a hospital this very minute. FBI agent Ritsema needs to conclude his investigation which includes interviewing you. It'll only be a few minutes more and we'll carry you to the chopper."

ALONG THE LEWIS CHANNEL, YELLOWSTONE NATIONAL PARK, WYOMING

Standing together where the body lay, Carrie looked toward where Beth and Drew were carrying Gretchen on a stretcher toward the medical helicopter. They would be taking Gretchen to the Jackson hospital for observation and any necessary treatment. Beth was walking next to the stretcher. Bringing her eyes back to look directly at Parker, who was standing next to her, Carrie said, "Alex and I need to leave soon. We need to arrive at the Jackson hospital before Gretchen. I told Drew to fly more slowly than usual and to not fly directly to the hospital. By the way, the Jackson hospital has a large helipad on the roof which accommodates at least three choppers. Before we leave, let's summarize what we believe happened here. Parker, you have been here all the time. Please tell us what you and Beth, plus Margaret, Wilma and Bruce did, what was concluded, and why.

"Okay," replied Parker. "First, we found no gun. Logic says the gun would be close to the shooter. We found no gun by the body. We concluded Aaron was not the shooter. Second, we drew conclusions based on the wounds, gun powder residue, and powder burns. Aaron was shot from a very close distance. His wound told us that. The shooter was standing very close to him. This would result in a great deal of gun powder residue and powder burn on the shooting hand of the shooter. Bruce did gun powder residue and powder burn tests on the two hands of Aaron. The results weren't definite. After talking through alternatives, we concluded while there was some residue on Aaron's right hand, along with minor powder burns, there wasn't enough of either to conclude Aaron shot Gretchen or himself. This is one of the weak links for us. Some residue and burns on Aaron's right hand, but not enough in our collective opinion. Consequently, we concluded Aaron didn't shoot anyone. Obviously, we then turned our attention to Gretchen. Another thing was where and how many shell casings we found. After finding the body and making sure Gretchen wasn't in serious condition, Beth and I examined the area around the body. I found one shell casing. Only one. This was before Gretchen told us her account of the shootings. After hearing Gretchen's account, I did another search. Gretchen confirmed the number of shots Beth and I heard. We heard two shots, one a few minutes after the other. I looked and looked for another shell casing. I didn't find one anywhere near the body. Unexpectedly, I found one near where Beth and I found Gretchen. From this, I concluded someone fired a gun very near to that spot. Finally, back to gun powder residue and powder burns. There was gun powder residue and burns on Gretchen's hands. The amount of gun powder residue and powder burns on Gretchen's right hand which, by the way, Gretchen herself told us was her dominant hand, was substantial. The amount suggested she shot a gun multiple times."

"So, if I can summarize, the conclusion you all reached from the evidence was that Gretchen shot Aaron and then shot herself. She shot herself to make it look like she had been shot by Aaron trying to run away from him. Is that how you see it? Do I have it correct?" asked Carrie.

"Yeah, you do." answered Parker. "I recognize our conclusions must be considered preliminary for two reasons. The matter of some gun powder residue and power burns on both Aaron and Gretchen's hands, more so on Gretchen's but, nevertheless, some on Aaron's hand. Also, no gun or bullets."

"You're right, Parker, not having the gun and bullets limits any conclusion. Also, why does Aaron have some gun powder residue and powder burns on his hand if he didn't shoot Gretchen, let alone himself?

Was it still there from shooting Professor Boersma? And don't forget Marlene. There are some holes in your conclusions. Not to say they are wrong. Only to say they aren't solid. There is no solid proof Gretchen shot anyone. For the moment, let's assume she did," said Carrie. "We need to do two things to solidify Gretchen being the shooter. One, we need to find the bullets. I assume the bullets are around here somewhere since they passed through both the body and Gretchen's thigh. as Wilma and Margaret's examinations determined. We also need to find the gun. Assuming Gretchen is the shooter, she would probably have thrown it somewhere. My bet is the Channel. Unfortunately, the water in the Channel moves rapidly so the gun would probably be swept along to who knows where. If she threw the gun into the shrubbery, would you be able to spend time looking for it? If you don't find it, we'll have a team come and go into the Channel. What I fear is that the current swept the gun into Lewis Lake which means there is very little chance of ever finding it."

"Okay. Carrie and I need to leave," said Alex. "Even with questions still lingering, I say we have enough evidence to place Gretchen under arrest for murder. We will wait until the doctors tell us we can take her into custody. Parker, in the meantime, can you stay here and do a careful search of the shrubbery for the gun?"

"I certainly can and will," responded Parker.

"Thanks, Parker. We need to get going," said Alex. "We need to turn the chopper around and come back equipped with a body bag. I'll have one of our techs come back on the chopper and accompany the body to the morgue in Jackson. I will contact Janet and bring her up to speed while we are on the chopper."

"Parker, while you are looking for the gun please also look for bullets," said Carrie. "They are out there somewhere. Okay Alex, let's go."

SECURITY OFFICE, ADMINISTRATION BUILDING, HEADQUARTERS YELLOWSTONE NATIONAL PARK, MAMMOTH, MONTANA

This could be big. I need to tell Bruce. I hope he is somewhere where his mobile will connect. She pushed the call button for Bruce Terpstra. She was greeted with the message that the number was not available. *I was afraid of this. No connection. I can't even leave a message. I'll try again in a few minutes. Do I dare contact Janet VanKampen? Bruce said she was sending two agents to the scene where Bruce was or possibly still is. I'm sure she can contact her agents who can then tell Bruce. I don't want to be left holding the bag with this information. It could prove to be vital.* She pushed the call button for the Billings office of the FBI.

"You have reached the Billings office of the FBI. How may I help you?"

"This is Ruth Boonstra of Yellowstone Security. You may remember I'm the Assistant to the Director. Director Bruce Terpstra is my boss. I have tried to reach Director Terpstra with some information I believe has an important bearing on the shootings your office and ours are investigating in Yellowstone. Director Terpstra isn't available by phone. I assume he's out of our carrier's network coverage. I know two of your agents are with Director Terpstra or at least they were. Maybe they have left. I felt those agents, if they had information, could pass it on to Director Terpstra."

"Ruth, for the moment, Janet is free. Rather than tell me and then I repeat it to her, you can tell her directly. Hold on please. I'll transfer your call to her."

OFFICE OF THE FBI, BILLINGS, MONTANA

I need to tell Parker this information before I contact Carrie and Alex. I believe they are on their way, with the suspected shooter, to the Jackson hospital, so I can't reach them for a while. Parker was the first person with authority on the scene of the shooting. He'll certainly have to be in court should there be a trial. First things first. Carrie and Alex need to know this information since they are now leading the investigation. I'll call them after I talk with Parker. Accessing the satellite phone number Parker had given her, she punched the call prompt and waited for him to answer.

"Hi, Janet. I saw it was you calling. I assume you're wanting an update from the scene here since Carrie and Alex have no doubt told you about what they've done. They are heading for Jackson. The body is on the way to the morgue in Jackson. The chopper left here with the body only a few minutes ago."

"Yes, I talked earlier with Carrie and Alex so I know what they did, where they are headed, and what they intend to do. I need to talk with them again and give them some information. I want you to have this information as well. It's the reason I'm calling. Carrie said you're the only person still at the scene. That makes it doubly important you have this information. The importance of finding the gun and the bullets has tripled. I know you and the others already looked for them. Please do it again. The case may depend on finding them."

"Janet, I know finding the gun and bullets has always been important. Why have the gun and bullets taken on increased importance? We all concluded Gretchen was the shooter. The evidence shows that. She then shot herself to make it look like the guy had shot her. Is that conclusion now being questioned? Why?"

"Let me tell you the information I have. Then you tell me if your conclusion changes."

He hadn't walked more than a few feet on both sides of where the body had lain when the satellite phone had signaled an incoming call. Thinking it would probably be Beth calling with an update on the situation in Jackson, he hadn't bothered to first check the calling number before answering. He had to hide his disappointment when we saw the caller was not Beth but Janet. After she told him the information Bruce Terpstra's assistant had told her, he realized he needed to contact Beth and alert her to this new information. Their conversation was brief because she wanted to accompany Gretchen to the FBI office in Jackson. Carrie and Alex were taking her there to officially charge her with the murder of Aaron Vogelzang. Beth told him she was contemplating hiring a lawyer for Gretchen, especially now in light of the information Parker had provided.

Finding bullets and the gun had taken on increased importance. *I'm here and everyone else is somewhere else. If bullets and the gun are to be found, I'm the person who needs to find them. I wish I had one of those metal detector things you see people use on beaches to search for coins or jewelry dropped by people. I bet Janet has one, but it does me no good since it's in Billings and not here. I have to find the bullets and the gun the old fashioned way, with my eyes while I crawl slowly on my hands and knees.* Crawling ever so slowly, he knew he couldn't allow his mind to wander. He needed to keep his focus on his task at hand. Those bullets had to be somewhere not too far from where the body had been.

OFFICE OF THE FBI, JACKSON, WYOMING

At the end of her conversation with her cousin, Gretchen's father, Beth had been asked by him to contact Connie DeVries, a criminal defense lawyer whom Gretchen's father knew. Beth had contacted her and she was now with Gretchen and Beth in a small conference room in the Jackson office of the FBI. Connie was diminutive in stature pushing five feet in height and weighing no more than one hundred pounds. What she lacked in size she more than made up in aggressiveness and intimidation. She wore a black turtleneck, jeans, and black pointed-toe boots. Beth didn't see any jewelry or rings. Beth guessed her age to be mid-fifties. Her overall impression was that she was not someone to mess with and she would leave no prisoners. Gretchen's father had told Beth that Connie had a reputation for being ruthless with a no-holds-barred approach in defending her clients. Beth wondered if that meant Connie would stop at nothing in defending Gretchen.

Carrie and Alex were in the next room. They had left the room while Beth and Gretchen remained, after Connie told them she was representing Gretchen and wanted to talk to her in private. Prior to requesting a private meeting with Gretchen, Connie had requested an explanation of the charge against Gretchen and the evidence supporting that charge. Armed with that information, she instructed Gretchen to not answer any questions or talk with anyone without Connie being present. Gretchen had insisted Beth was an exception. When Connie told Carrie and Alex that Gretchen and she required a place to talk in private, Gretchen insisted Beth join them. "The FBI's evidence is the location of two shell casings, gun powder residue and powder burns on your right hand, and an insignificant amount on the hands of the male victim whom Gretchen says was the shooter. Let me add here my understanding is that the residue and burn tests were done by a person whom, I suspect, isn't certified to conduct such tests. Without a certified person on site overseeing the tests being performed, the results can be brought into question. There was no such certified person present. Furthermore, the tests were done in a non-secure environment. The tests were performed outdoors in a field where the elements could have impacted the results. Another factor is that no bullets and no gun have been found. Without bullets and especially without a gun, the shell casings don't amount to much of anything. Finally, there is no witness. No gun; no bullets; no witness; questionable gun powder residue and powder burn tests. Bottom line, the FBI has a very weak case."

"What are you telling us? Are you suggesting the evidence won't hold up in court?", asked Beth.

"Juries are funny animals," responded Connie. "Especially in a murder trial. In criminal cases, such as a murder case, all it takes is one juror to vote not guilty and the trial is over. The defendant is not guilty as charged. My experience is that juries are reluctant to find a defendant guilty unless the evidence is so overwhelming and air tight that there is absolutely no question about the guilt of the defendant. I don't see a strong case no matter what the charge might be, especially if the charge is first or second degree murder. Don't misunderstand. I'm not claiming I'm a never-lose-a-case defense lawyer. I don't like to lose. I never intend to lose. I can see some ways to attack the FBI's findings. I repeat. No gun. No bullets. No witness. Questionable tests. Can we persuade at least one juror to vote 'not guilty'? It is always a crap shoot."

"How quickly can you get me out of this nightmare? I'm innocent," said Gretchen. "I told everyone I was innocent. I explained over and over again how Aaron shot the professor and then me. No one, other than Aunt Beth, believed me. Finally someone believes me besides Aunt Beth."

"I didn't say I believe you," responded Connie. "I'm not into believing or not believing. What I'm into is providing the best defense I can, given the evidence presented by the prosecution and contradictory evidence I can provide. My job is to defend you as best I can and seek to win your acquittal."

Directing her question to Connie, Beth asked, "Connie, whatever Gretchen tells you is covered by attorney-client privilege, correct? And you can't divulge it to anyone even if a court or judge orders you to do so, correct?"

"With a few exceptions, you are correct, Beth," replied Connie. "The attorney-client privilege has been challenged all the way to the Supreme Court. As Gretchen's attorney, anything she tells me is privileged. Even if she lies to me, I can't divulge to anyone her lie unless that lie resulted in a crime." Pointing her finger directly at Gretchen and in a strong tone of voice she continued, "Of course, if you lie to me and I know you are lying or I find out you lied to me, I'll drop you so fast it'll make your head spin. Even if the truth will harm our case, tell me the truth anyway. I'm obligated to provide you with the strongest defense I can muster and I will do so regardless of what you did or did not do. The exception is if you lie to me."

"What if I tell you I've already lied? Would you drop me? I didn't lie to you but, and I'm not saying I did, but I'm asking if I lied to someone and told you I did, my telling you is privileged, correct? You also wouldn't drop me because I lied to someone else but not you, correct?"

"Whatever you tell me is privileged, period. Only a few exceptions exist to that fact. Remember, this is a two-way street. You can drop me at anytime with no reasons given. That's your prerogative. I won't drop you because of what you tell me, as long as it's the truth. I don't mean if someone lied to you and you told me that lie thinking it was the truth. I mean you lie to me knowing what you are telling me is a lie. Then I will drop you. Do you have something you want to tell me?"

For several seconds Gretchen stared away from Beth and Connie. She was obviously contemplating her response. *She's torn,* Beth thought. *She wants to come clean with Connie but she also doesn't want to. If I leave she and Connie alone, she might be more inclined to give Connie the straight scoop.* Taking advantage of Gretchen's indecision and the silence, Beth said, "I'm going to step out and leave the two of you alone. I'll be somewhere in the office so I won't be far." Leaving the room, she closed the door behind her, wondering what Gretchen was poised to tell Connie.

ALONG THE LEWIS CHANNEL, YELLOWSTONE NATIONAL PARK, WYOMING

Sitting on a flat-top boulder, he had an internal debate focused on his responsibilities. He wondered if his responsibilities should be considered in a priority order. He felt his first priority was being loyal to the U.S. Department of the Interior and Yellowstone National Park. The second priority was to the Crow Indian Tribe and its heritage. The third to Western historical heritage and the legacy of John Colter. A distant fourth, in his mind, was to the American public. *Maybe these priorities aren't the ones I should be considering. Certainly, there are others. Does it really make much difference what the priorities are? Should I be thinking about priorities at all?* Debating with oneself wasn't very productive, he concluded. There didn't seem to be a clear answer, at least not one he could decipher. Although he was pleased his search for bullets had been successful, he doubted the one he found would provide any additional information beyond that which Janet had already shared with him. The bullet was mashed beyond being informative regarding how the shooting had happened. The bullet had been mashed when it apparently struck the rocks around which he had found it. He could envision the bullet passing through the body of Aaron and crashing against rocks. Regardless how it ended up where it had, without the gun from which it was fired, only the manufacturer of the bullet could be identified. He suspected thousands upon thousands of such bullets had been manufactured, distributed, and sold across the country. Even if the bullet he found could be traced to the seller, from there it would be a guessing game as to the buyer. Even then, the buyer could be a volume purchaser, such as law enforcement or the military, which made tracing the bullet to a single person impossible.

The disposition of the bullet wasn't what he was debating with himself. He knew what to do with the bullet. He would give it to Janet. She would add it to the evidence already in the possession of the FBI. The bullet would be added to the gun power residue and powder burn test results, entry and exit wounds on the body, location of the shell casings, and the testimony of Marlene VanderBrink. Marlene had testified that she believed a woman shot her when the door of the cabin opened. He also wasn't debating with himself the conclusions that Margaret, Wilma, Bruce, Carrie, Alex, and he had reached about Gretchen being the killer. He wasn't so sure where Beth stood on the conclusions but he knew she was more in their camp than she wasn't. Her judgment, he feared, was clouded by her blood relationship with Gretchen. Nevertheless, he was confident Beth understood and supported justice being done.

His debate with himself centered on what he now held in his hand. He was holding an odd shaped piece of rock with a chunk of something in it. The chunk, which was corroded and blackened, was about the size of a ping pong ball. He knew the story of John Colter and Chief Swift Eagle. The legend of Swift Eagle hiding pieces of rock with gold in them and giving John Colter a map showing the location of the pieces of rock had been a legend handed down from one generation of Crow tribal members to the next. He had heard the legend again from Gretchen, when they had questioned her about the reason she, and the guy she called Aaron, were in the Lewis Channel vicinity in the first place. What was this small rock he was holding in his hand? Was it one of Swift Eagle's hidden pieces of rock? Was the chunk gold? Whatever it was, how had it come to be partially buried among several small rocks? Maybe it wasn't buried at all. Maybe it was nothing more than one of the millions and millions of small rocks throughout Yellowstone. Maybe the chunk in the rock was quartz, feldspar, or some naturally occurring mineral. The only way to find out would be to hold onto the rock, have it cleaned, and then analyzed. Trying to decide whether to do that or not was what he was debating with himself.

If, and it's a big if, if this piece of rock contains gold, I'll be questioned as to where I found it until the cows come home. Regardless of my answer, whether true or false, the area surrounding the location I identify will turn into a chaotic mess. Hordes of treasure seekers, lawyers, Native American advocates, environmentalists, U.S. Government officials, newspaper reporters, news network reporters, and just plain old curiosity seekers will descend on the area. If I tell the truth and identify the location as the Lewis Channel, this area of Yellowstone will never be the same. It will be devastated beyond recognition. Furthermore, if Yellowstone moved to protect the area and make it a no trespassing zone, while the exploration was underway and lawyers argued and debated the ownership of the pieces of rock, it would cost Yellowstone a great deal in personnel and dollars, neither of which Yellowstone could afford . And I bet I know who would get stuck with the task of establishing procedures and security measures and then having the hassle of implementing the rules and regulations. Beth would. Would that be fair to her? Do I want her to have to deal with all that? On the other hand, what are my obligations and responsibilities to the Interior Department and Yellowstone National Park? To the Crow Tribe? To the legacy of Swift Eagle or John Colter? What should I do?

ONE WEEK LATER
GOLD MEDAL FLY
FISHING SHOP, WEST
YELLOWSTONE, MONTANA

The inventory of Sage fly fishing rods and reels along with Simms waders, wading boots, jackets, and shirts needed an infusion of products in anticipation of increased sales. More and more clients were relying on the Gold Medal Fly Fishing Shop to supply their fly fishing needs. The inventory needed to keep up with demand. Lori and Parker were deciding which products to order from Sage and Simms respectively when Parker's mobile phone chirped. Looking at the phone's screen, he saw the call was from Beth. "Hi, Beth. It's good to hear from you. Are you still in Jackson? I haven't tried to contact you since you and Gretchen went to Jackson. I assumed you've been up to your eyeballs in legal matters."

"It's good to hear your voice too," said Beth. "I apologize for not calling you before now. You don't have to explain why you didn't try to contact me. You're right. I've been busy with Gretchen's legal matters. I've been involved with all the give and take related to the case against her. Before I tell you the latest, I want you to know I'm still trying to digest it all myself. I might come across as not having all the info."

"By the hesitation in your voice, something tells me I'm not going to like what you're about to tell me," replied Parker. "I have this feeling you have bad news."

"Bad. Good. Depends how you view what I'm going to tell you. Since you raised the bad/good comparison, let me ask you some questions. Do you believe in our judicial system where a person is innocent until proven guilty? Does evidence still trump coincidence or possibility? Is reasonable doubt sufficient to render a not guilty verdict?"

"Beth, you knew my answers before you even asked. Of course I believe in our judicial system, as flawed as it is. Absolutely, a person is innocent until proven guilty. That's at the heart of our judicial system. Why do you ask?"

"Because, as you know, all of us, myself included but with some hesitation, concluded Gretchen shot Professor Boersma and Aaron. We had Gretchen guilty of two murders. Add shooting and wounding Marlene to the murders."

"Yeah, that's how I saw it. Shooting Marlene and murdering two people."

"Well Parker, are you ready for this?"

"Ready for what?"

"Ready to be shocked. Ready for some disbelief. Maybe you should sit down"

"Now you really have me wondering what's going on. Go ahead, let me hear it."

"The FBI has dropped all charges against Gretchen. Everything. She's a free woman. Janet informed Connie DeVries only a little while ago. Janet said there was not convincing evidence to support a charge of murder. Ditto for a charge of shooting a federal employee. She stated to Connie they, meaning the FBI, didn't believe Gretchen's story but, at the same time, weren't able to refute it."

He tried to process what Beth was saying. *How can this be? What happened to change Janet's mind?* "I don't understand," said Parker. "I thought the gun powder residue and powder burn results were clinchers. Who else but Gretchen could have shot those people?"

"I'm not the person to ask those questions let alone try to answer them. Janet is. She made the decision to drop the charges. She must have had good reasons to do so. Do yourself and me a favor. Ask Janet to explain her reasoning. After you talk with her, please call me and tell me what you learned."

"I'm still perplexed. What different evidence or new information caused Janet to drop the case? It doesn't make sense."

"I don't want to be the middle person between you and Janet. I might describe incorrectly what she told Connie, who then told Gretchen, who then told me. I'm hearing it third hand. You know how details can change when passed from one person to another. Talk to Janet. Hear it unfiltered, directly from the horse's mouth."

"Okay, I will. Thanks for calling and giving me a heads up." Ending the call he immediately found the number of the Billings FBI Office.

"You've reached the Billings office of the FBI. How may I assist you?

"Alice, it's Parker. Is Janet there? It's important I speak with her."

"I'm sorry, Parker, she's in Jackson at our office there. I assume she'll be calling in later. I'll tell her you called."

"Do you think she'll mind if I call her mobile? I really do need to talk with her."

"Seeing it's you, I doubt she'll mind. She usually doesn't accept calls on her mobile but you aren't a usual person given your status with us. Go ahead and give it a try. If she doesn't answer, call me back and I'll call her. She almost always answers my calls."

"Thanks, Alice. I'll try her mobile." Ending the call with Alice, he scrolled down his contacts list to Janet and pressed the call prompt. After a few rings, Janet answered.

"I was wondering how long it would be before you called me," said Janet. "I was going to call you earlier but I got tied up in some tricky legal matters."

"Beth told me you dropped the charges against Gretchen. Nothing more. She said I should hear the reasons for your decision unfiltered. In other words, straight from you. I can't believe it. Tell me what happened to cause you to drop all the charges."

"Fair enough. During my first conversation with Carrie and Alex, they expressed concern about the strength of the evidence. We, I'm including myself with Carrie and Alex, have been involved with enough criminal cases to know when evidence is strong or weak. The evidence we had to begin with was weak. It only became weaker over time. The forensic folks in our Denver lab advised us the tests of the gun powder residue and powder burns conducted by Bruce had been done in a haphazard and unsecured manner. I'm not criticizing Bruce. He worked with what he had and under conditions which he couldn't control. No fault of his. However, a good defense lawyer would know enough to bring at least one expert to provide testimony showing how tests conducted in the field, by an uncertified tester and using outdated equipment, could be faulty. The key words are could be. Another way of saying could be is reasonable doubt. Reasonable doubt. The two words that are the kiss of death for any criminal trial."

"Wait a minute," replied Parker. "The gun powder residue and powder burn tests were conclusive. There was an insignificant amount on Aaron's hands. Contrary to that result was the result for Gretchen. A whole lot on Gretchen's right hand, her dominate hand. What's faulty about that?"

"Nothing on the surface," replied Janet, "and possibly nothing at all. Remember, the equipment Bruce used is obsolete. Also, the conditions under which the tests were conducted --outdoor, wind, sun, humidity -- might have contaminated the equipment. The key word is might. Said another way, reasonable doubt. Plus, and this isn't a knock against Bruce, the tests were conducted by a person not certified to perform such tests. The forensic and techie people said a good defense attorney would raise enough doubt about the results to render them essentially useless as evidence."

"What about Marlene VanderBrink's testimony? She remembered being shot by a woman," replied Parker. "Gretchen was the only women in the cabin. Liz had gone to the Crow reservation. Gretchen had to shoot Marlene."

"I agree, believe me I do. But I can't allow my personal belief to replace criminal proceedings and law. Carrie, Alex, and I had to think how Marlene's testimony would hold up in front of a jury. Remember, reasonable doubt is the killer of most criminal cases. Several matters with Marlene's memory are troublesome. One, there is no witness. It is Marlene's word against Gretchen's. Gretchen says she was standing next to Aaron in the cabin. Aaron had a gun pointed at Gretchen and threatened her if she didn't open the door. When Gretchen opened the door, Marlene would've seen her for a second or two before Aaron shot her. Plausible? You and I might not think so but one or two jurors might think just the opposite. Yes, plausible. Again, no witness. Marlene testified she remembered a woman opened the door but she can't be one hundred percent sure the woman shot her. She can't deny the possibility a person next to or standing behind the woman shot her. In other words, reasonable doubt. I agreed with Carrie and Alex's assessment that Marlene's testimony isn't definitive enough to conclude, without a reasonable doubt, Gretchen shot Marlene. Reasonable doubt raises its ugly head again."

"I'm beginning to get a sense why you felt you had a weak case," said Parker. "Having no gun and a bullet so mashed to be of no use doesn't help either."

"Speaking of a gun. Along with your search, my underwater team searched the Lewis Channel all the way to Lewis Lake and then from Lewis Lake to Lewis Falls. No gun. Gretchen says her anxiety level was so high and she was so panicked she can't remember anything about a gun. Convenient loss of memory, huh? Anyway, the testimony Betsy Slager provided made the case even weaker. I call it gun by proxy. Betsy Slager testified she gave Aaron the key to the gun locker in the Canyon Ranger Station. When her testimony was checked, we discovered a thirty-nine caliber handgun missing along with some thirty-nine caliber ammunition. The shell casings match the ammunition taken from the Canyon Ranger Station. Circumstantial for sure but a possible conclusion is the gun was taken by Aaron and he used it to kill Professor Boersma and shoot Marlene and Gretchen. We believe Aaron possessed the gun at one point in time. Did he use it to do the shootings? No witness to say he didn't. One witness to say he did."

"Yeah, after you told me about Marlene's recollection of her being shot at the cabin, I wondered if it might be challenged. You never found anyone to collaborate her story, correct?"

"We contacted all the visitors for that day who were occupants of cabins in the vicinity of Cabin 17. No one saw anything except the woman who heard a vehicle drive past her cabin after she heard the shot. She then decided to investigate. Thankfully she did. Her intervention probably saved Marlene's life. No one saw who shot Marlene. No witness. Marlene's questionable memory versus Gretchen's story. Both plausible. More reasonable doubt."

"Janet, you're right. Reasonable doubt. Weak case for sure. I must ask, did the bullet and shell casings help the case or have no effect?"

"As you know the bullet was mashed. It would have been impossible to link it to a particular gun. As it was, we had no gun anyway. The bullet did tell us the caliber of the gun which, we found out, was the caliber of the gun we believe Aaron stole from the Canyon Ranger Station. The location of the shell casings, which you found, actually contributed to Gretchen's account of how the shootings happened and why the shell casings were located where you found them."

"You're telling me," replied Parker, "the location of the shell casings give credence to Gretchen's version of the shootings? I thought they did just the opposite. I thought their location blew a hole in her story."

"Initially they did or we thought they did. Then Gretchen changed her story. She told Connie she lied to all of you. The question to which we'll never know the answer is one Connie will never tell us or anyone else for that matter because of attorney-client privilege. Did Connie coach Gretchen into giving a different story including a different set of events surrounding the shooting? In other words, did Connie fashion a defense and then coach Gretchen into confessing, and I use that word cautiously, to conform to what Connie fashioned?"

"Okay, lay it on me. Gretchen's so-called confession or whatever it should be called. Her different story. What is it?"

"You're already aware of the uncertainty of Gretchen shooting Marlene. Gretchen says Aaron shot Marlene. Gretchen says Aaron had a gun pointed at her and ordered her to open the door. Next, she says Aaron shot Professor Boersma when he tried to divert Aaron's attention enough to overpower him.

"I bet I can finish her story," said Parker. "She took off running and Aaron shot her, the bullet passing through her thigh. But, how did the shell casing end up by Gretchen some thirty yards or so from Aaron's body?"

"Gretchen said she lied about how she was shot. She said Aaron didn't shoot her as she was running away."

"Janet, we know Gretchen was shot through her thigh. We know Aaron was shot at close range. We never found a gun. We found one shell casing by Aaron's body and one by Gretchen, some thirty yards or so away from the body. I know you're going to explain how this happened different from how Gretchen first explained it to us which, as you know, none of us bought. Gretchen's story meant Aaron shot himself which didn't make sense to us and the evidence didn't support it."

"The most significant and impactful changes in her account occurred when she, through her attorney Connie, told us how the shell casings were where you found them. I've been thinking ever since Connie told me, certainly before I decided to drop the charges, how to punch holes in her new story. I asked Carrie and Alex to do the same. We weren't able to come up with anything which would convince a juror Gretchen was telling another lie. I'm convinced she lied but I'm also convinced we couldn't prove it."

"Would it be possible to ask a judge to order an investigation into whether Connie compromised her oath as an attorney? Instead of showing Gretchen lied, show Connie influenced her to lie. Same outcome,"

"If there had been a trial, perhaps the presiding judge might have considered rendering such a declaration from the bench about investigating Connie's actions on behalf of her client. However, prior to a trial, a client and his or her attorney can discuss anything they wish with no accountability of the attorney. Remember, attorney-client privilege. No way to prove Connie acted improperly."

"Too bad. I struck out again. So, what is Gretchen's new story?"

"I know I'm repeating myself several times over. It isn't that I believe your intelligence level or ability to understand the law are not up to speed. It's because reasonable doubt is so critical in judging whether an argument will be so airtight that doubt has no way to creep in."

"I'm not offended at all by being continually reminded of the reasonable doubt cornerstone of our judicial system. I 'll keep it in mind as you fire away."

"Okay. Here's what Connie said Gretchen told her. No witness to the conversation and with attorney-client privilege who knows what, if anything, Gretchen actually said to Connie or what, if anything, Connie actually said to Gretchen. In other words, who said what to whom we'll never know."

"I don't like it but I fully understand," replied Parker. "What's the bottom line?"

"The bottom line is Gretchen told Connie she, Gretchen, shot Aaron in self defense because he had threatened to kill her. According to her story, he had looked away from her for a brief moment when a wolf howled close by. As a sidebar, we checked and there is a wolf den in that area. Going on, she claims she used the distraction caused by the wolf howl to try and get the gun away from him. They struggled and the gun went off. She says that was the shot that wounded her leg. She said she screamed and was able to knee him in his crotch. As he bent over, she wrestled the gun from him and pulled the trigger which was the shot that killed him. She panicked. Wanting to get away, she took off limping but wasn't able to make it very far before she collapsed because of the pain in her leg. She was so distraught she wasn't thinking straight. Again, her story, not mine. She is adamant in saying she doesn't remember or know, but she thinks the shell casing from one of the two shots when she and Aaron were struggling may have caught in her clothing and then dropped onto the ground where you found it after she collapsed."

"You really aren't kidding, are you? You're serious. Aaron was shot during a struggle with her which also had her being shot in the leg. And she was so distraught and driven by panic she limped for about thirty yards or so with a shell casing in her clothes which just happened to fall onto the ground when she stopped limping and collapsed. Plus, in her heightened state of anxiety, she has no recollection what happened to the gun. She doesn't remember throwing the gun into Lewis Channel or into the nearby shrubbery or down a muskrat hole or maybe into that wolf den that you told me about. How convenient.

"Nice summary," said Janet. "I couldn't do better myself."

"Her story explains the two shots Beth and I heard and how gun powder residue and powder burns were on her right hand. It explains how one shell casing was by the body and the other by her. Not bad as far as making an explanation to fit the facts."

"Believe me, Parker, it makes me sick. Two people dead. Shot by Gretchen. But, I say it again. Reasonable doubt. Reasonable doubt. No witnesses. Can you objectively say that there isn't a possibility a juror might find her story plausible and thus have reasonable doubt about the charges against her? No one exists to cast doubt on her story. No witnesses to refute any of her cock and bull explanations. No evidence to refute her account of what took place. The evidence which does exist can be interpreted in differing ways which translates into reasonable doubt."

Shaking his head he said, "A murderer walks free. Justice is mocked. A sad day for sure."

BIG TIMBER RESTAURANT, GARDINER, MONTANA

"Talk about mixed feelings. I'm happy for my cousin and his family but I'm alarmed and angry that a murderer is walking free with no penalty for her treachery," said Beth. "I'm sick about my participation in having Gretchen go free. I wanted so much to believe she was innocent."

"The evidence we thought would bring a conviction did a whole lot of good, didn't it? Don't beat yourself up over how all this turned out," said Parker. "You didn't change the outcome. I, too, am angry when I think about how Gretchen and her attorney changed Gretchen's story to take advantage of the weak areas in the case and used the law to obscure the truth. How can Connie DeVries continue to practice law knowing she manipulated her client and helped her escape justice and the rightful penalty for her actions? I can't stand thinking about it anymore. Let's try and put it behind us and not talk about it anymore starting now."

"I'll try if you will help me," replied Beth.

"I need your help too," said Parker, "but with a totally different matter. I've struggled with it ever since I made a discovery when I was searching for the gun and bullets. I'm sorry I had to refer to the shootings but it's necessary to set the context for what I'm going to show you." He handed the piece of rock with the blackened and corroded chunk in it across the table to her.

Turning it over in her hand, she said, "This sure is something I haven't seen before. What is this?"

"That's what I need your help figuring out. No, let me say it another way. What you're holding in your hand could be a rock with gold in it. Even though it's blackened and corroded, when you rub it long enough, as I did with that corner, it becomes a lighter color, as you can see. It may not be gold. It might only be a rock with some quartz, feldspar, or some other mineral in it. I found it when I was searching for the bullets. I realize this is a stretch but it might be one of Swift Eagle's pieces of rock with gold in it."

"What? Are you pulling my leg? You think this is gold? One of Swift Eagle's pieces of rock?"

"As I said, I don't know," replied Parker. "Maybe. Maybe not. My question to you is what should I do? Keep it quiet and let the legend of Swift Eagle, John Colter, and hidden pieces of rock with gold in them buried in Yellowstone continue or have this piece of rock analyzed with the results made public and let the consequences come as they may? What if the chunk is gold? Is the world ready for another gold rush that would destroy a significant portion of Yellowstone? Do we want, who knows how many lawyers, to argue ownership rights for several years? What is the Crow Tribe owed and due? Does any agency, group, or individual actually end up benefiting? In the end, there can be only one winner and a whole lot of losers. Is that the best outcome?"

EPILOGUE

A WOLF DEN IN THE AREA OF LEWIS LAKE AND THE LEWIS CHANNEL
YELLOWSTONE NATIONAL PARK, WYOMING

The pups were becoming more restless and more difficult to control with each passing day. Soon they would be too big for all of them to live comfortably together in the den. If only she could move those pieces of rock to the back of the den. More room for her family and especially for the growing pups. She had tried unsuccessfully to push the pieces of rock with her nose and move them with her front paws during the time she was giving birth and caring for several litters of pups. She had thought about finding a new den but this one was so well hidden and protected she wasn't sure she would find another so well situated. Her pack controlled the region along Lewis Lake, Lewis Channel, and the Lewis River, as well as the immediate area surrounding the den. Her pack had been successful in fighting off other packs. She had been able to hunt with her pack while her pups were watched over and protected by others of her pack who weren't primary hunters. The recent activity of humans and the monsters from the sky had driven her and the pups as deep into the den as they could go for a substantial period of time. Her pack had scattered to avoid confrontation with the humans.

Even with the scent of blood strong in the air, it wasn't a familiar scent. Not from an elk or bison carcass. She had wanted to investigate the source of the scent but held back. The presence of the hated humans, whose scent was even stronger than the scent of the blood, kept her from investigating. The scents were now gone. The quiet of the day was back, broken only by the yipping of the pups and the sounds of water rushing over rocks.

One of the pups scampered past with a small piece of the hard rock in its teeth. A play thing for the pups. She could see a dark colored chunk of something in the rock. A few days earlier, another pup had carried a similar piece of the hard rock from the den. All the pups had played with it and then immediately forgot about it when a flock of ducks had landed on the water drawing their attention. Maybe this was the way to empty the den of the pieces of rock. Let the pups carry them from the den and use them as playthings.

Made in the USA
San Bernardino, CA
30 November 2017